the LONG view

a novel by FLETCHER PRATT

MORE WILDSIDE CLASSICS

the LONG view

a novel by FLETCHER PRATT

WILDSIDE PRESS

THE LONG VIEW

Originally published in the December, 1952 issue of *Startling Stories* magazine. Copyright © 1952 by Better Publications, Inc. Copyright not renewed. New elements copyright © 2005 by Wildside Press.

Published by:

Wildside Press, LLC
www.wildsidepress.com

Wildside Pulp Classics
Series Editor: John Gregory Betancourt

INTRODUCTION
THE SILICONE WORLD

ON THE following pages are reproduced the author's notes on THE LONG VIEW. We are presenting them in article form not only because they supply to the interested reader an absorbing technical background to the novel, but because they form a revealing picture of the wheels and gears that click and whir in a stf author's mind when he really sets out to do a job—the exhaustive research and planning which he will undertake in order that the completed work will be solid as a rock. Fletcher Pratt speaking—

THE planet is named Uller (it seems that in interstellar travel the names of Norse gods, instead of Greek, were applied to the few habitable worlds). It is the second planet of the star Beta Hydri, right angle 0.23, declension -77:32; GO (solar) type star, of approximately the same size as the sun; distance from earth 21 light years.

Uller revolves around Beta Hydri in a nearly circular orbit, at a distance of 105,000,000 miles, making it a little colder than earth. A year is of the approximate length of that on earth. A day lasts 26 hours.

The axis of Uller is in the same plane as the orbit, so that at a certain time of the year the north pole is pointed directly at the sun, while at the opposite end of the orbit, it points directly away. The result is highly exaggerated seasons. At the poles the temperature runs from 120° C. to a low of −80° C. At the equator it remains not far from plus 10° C. all year round. Strong winds during the summer and winter, from the hot to the cold pole. Few winds during the spring and fall. The appearance of the poles varies during the year from baked deserts to glaciers covered with solid CO_2. Free water exists in the equatorial regions all year round.

2. SOLAR MOVEMENT AS SEEN FROM ULLER.

As seen from the north pole—no sun visible on Jan. 1. On April 1, it bisects the horizon all day, swinging completely around. April 1 to July 1, it continues swinging around, gradually rising in the sky, the spiral converging to its center at the zenith, which it reaches on July 1. From July to October 1 the spiral starts again, spreading out from the center until on October 1 it bisects the horizon again. On October 1 night arrives again and stays until April 1.

At the equator, the sun is visible bisecting the southern horizon for all 26 hours of the day on January 1. From January 1 to April 1 the sun starts to dip below the horizon at night, to rise higher above it during the day. During all this time it rises and sets at the same hours, but rises in the southeast and sets in the southwest. At noon it is higher each day in the southern sky, until April 1, when it rises due east, passes through the zenith and sets due east. From April 1 to July 1, its noon position drops down to the north until on July 1, it is visible all day, bisected by the northern horizon.

3. CHEMISTRY AND GEOLOGY OF ULLER.

Calcium and chlorine are rarer than on earth; sodium is somewhat commoner. As a result of the shortage of calcium there is a higher ratio of silicates to carbonates than exists on earth. The water is slightly alkaline, and resembles a very dilute solution of sodium silicate (water glass). It would have a pH of 8.5 and would taste slightly soapy. Also, when it dries out it leaves a sticky, and then a glassy, crackly film. Rocks look fairly earthlike, but the absence or scarcity of anything like limestone is noticeable. Practically all the sedimentary rocks are of the sandstone type.

4. ANIMAL LIFE.

Life developed as it did on earth, in the permanent waters, but because of the abundance of silicon, there was a strong tendency for the microscopic organisms to develop silicate exoskeletons, like diatoms. The present invertebrate animal life of the plant is of this type and is confined to the equatorial seas. They run from amoeba-like objects to things like crayfish, with silicate skeletons. Later, some species of these started taking the silicon into their soft tissues, and eventually their carbon-chain compounds were converted to silicone type chains, from

$$- \overset{|}{\underset{|}{C}} - \overset{|}{\underset{|}{C}} - \overset{|}{\underset{|}{C}} - \overset{|}{\underset{|}{C}} - \text{ to }$$

$$O - \overset{|}{\underset{|}{Si}} - O - \overset{|}{\underset{|}{Si}} - O - \overset{|}{\underset{|}{Si}}$$ with organic radicals on the side links. These organisms were a transitional type, with silicone tissues and water body fluids, resembling the earthly amphibians, and are now practically extinct. There are a few species, something like segmented worms, still to be seen in backwaters of the central seas.

A further development occurred when the silicone-chain animals began to get short-chain silicones into their circulatory systems, held in solution by OH or NH_2 groups on the ends and branches of the chains. The proportion of these compounds gradually increased until the water was a minor and then a missing

constituent. The larger mobile species, then, were practically anhydrous. Their blood consists of short-chain silicones, wtih quartz reinforcing, and their armor, teeth, etc., of pure amorphous quartz (opal). Most of these parts are of the milky variety, variously tinted with metallic impurities, as are the varieties of sapphires.

These pure silicone animals, due to their practical indestructibility, annihilated all but the smaller of the carbon animals, and drove the compromise types into odd corners as relics. They developed into a fish-like animal—with a very large swim-bladder to compensate for the rather higher density of the silicone tissues—and from these fish the land animals developed. Due to their high density and resulting high weight, they tend to be low to the ground, rather reptilian in look. Three pairs of legs are usual in order to distribute the heavy load. There is no sharp dividing line between the quartz armor and the silicone tissue. One merges into the other.

The dominant pure silicone animals only could become mobile and venture far from the temperate equatorial regions of Uller, for they alone were independent of the planet's violent climate, since they neither froze nor stiffened with cold, nor boiled off when it got really hot. Note that all animal life on this planet is cold-blooded, with a negligible difference between body and ambient temperatures. Since the animals are silicones, they don't get sluggish, like cold snakes.

5. PLANT LIFE.

The plants are of the carbon metabolism-silicate shell type, like the primitive animals. They spread out from the equator as far as they could go before the baking polar summers killed them. They had normal seasonal growth in the temperate zones, and remained dormant and frozen solid during the winter. At the poles there is no vegetation—not because of the cold winters, but because of the hot summers. The cold winter winds frequently blow over dead trees and roll them as far as the equatorial seas. Other dead vegetation, because of the highly silicious water, always gets petrified, like the petrified forest, unless it gets eaten first. What with the quartz-speckled hides of the living vegetation, and the solid quartz of the dead, a forest is spectacular.

The silicone animals live on the plants. They chomp them up, dehydrate them, and convert their silicious outer bark and carbonaceous interiors into silicones for themselves. When silicone tissue is metabolized, the carbon and hydrogen go to CO_2 and H_2O, which are breathed out, while the Silicon goes into SiO_2, which is deposited as more teeth and armor. (Compare the terrestrial octopus, which makes armor plating out of calcium urate instead of excreting urea or uric acid.) The animals can, of course, eat each other, too, or try to make a meal of the small carbonaceous animals of the equatorial seas.

Further note that the animals cannot digest plants when they are cold. They can eat them and store them, but the disposal of the solid water and CO_2 is too difficult a problem. When they warm up, the water in the plants melts and can be disposed of, and things are simpler.

All rivers are seasonal, running from the polar regions to the central seas in the spring only, or until the polar cap is completely dried out.

The Fluorine Planet

The planet named Niflheim is the fourth planet of Nu Puppis, right angle 6:36, declension -43:09; B8 type star, blue-white and hot, 148 light years distant from the earth, which will require a speed in excess of light to reach it.

Niflheim is 462,000,000 miles from its primary, a little less than the distance of Jupiter from our sun. It thus does not receive too great a total amount of energy, but what it does receive is of high potential, a large fraction of it being in the ultra-violet and higher frequencies. (Watch out for really super-special sunburn, etc., on unwarned personnel.)

The gravity of Niflheim is approximately 1 g, the atmospheric pressure approximately 1 atmosphere, and the average ambient temperature about -60° C; -70° F.

2. ATMOSPHERE.

The oxidizer in the atmosphere is free fluorine (F_2) in a rather low concentration, about 4 or 5 per cent. With it appears a mad collection of gases. There are a few inert diluants, such as N_2 (nitrogen), argon, helium, neon, &c., but the major fraction consists of CF_4 (carbon tetrafluoride), BF_3 "boron trifluoride), SiF_4 (Silicon tetrafluoride), PF_5 (phosphorous pentafluoride), SF_6 (sulphur hexafluoride) and probably others. In other words, the fluorides of all the non-metals that can form fluorides. The phosphorous pentafluoride rains out when the weather gets cold. There is also free oxygen, but no chlorine. That would be liquid except in very hot weather. It sometimes appears combined with fluorine in chlorine trifluoride. The atmosphere, on examination, has a slight yellowish tinge.

3. SOIL AND GEOLOGY.

Above the metallic core of the planet, the lithosphere consists exclusively of fluorides of the metals. There are no oxides, sulfides, silicates or chlorides. There are small deposits of such things as bromine trifluoride, but these have no great importance. Since fluorides are weak mechanically, the terrain is flattish. Nothing tough like granite to build mountains out of. Since the fluoride ion is colorless, the color of the soil depends upon the predominant metal in the region. As most of the light metals also have colorless ions, the colored rocks are rather rare.

7

4. THE WATERS UNDER THE EARTH.

They consist of liquid hydrofluoric acid (HF). It melts at -83° C. and boils at 19.4° C. In it are dissolved varying quantities of metallic and non-metallic fluorides, such as boron trifluoride, sodium fluoride, etc. When the oceans and lakes freeze, they do so from the bottom up, so there is no layer of ice over free liquid.

5. PLANTS AND PLANT METABOLISM.

The plants function by photosynthesis, taking HF as water from the soil, and carbon tetrafluoride as the equivalent of carbon dioxide from the air to produce chain compounds, such as:

$$-\overset{\displaystyle H}{\underset{\displaystyle F}{\overset{|}{\underset{|}{C}}}} - \overset{\displaystyle H}{\underset{\displaystyle F}{\overset{|}{\underset{|}{C}}}} - \overset{\displaystyle H}{\underset{\displaystyle F}{\overset{|}{\underset{|}{C}}}} - \overset{\displaystyle H}{\underset{\displaystyle F}{\overset{|}{\underset{|}{C}}}} -$$

and at the same time liberating free fluorine. This reaction could only take place on a planet receiving lots of ultraviolet because so much energy is needed to break up carbon tetrafluoride and hydrofluoric acid. The plant catalyst (doubling for the magnesium in chlorophyl) is nickel. The plants are colored in various ways. They get their metals from the soil.

5. ANIMALS AND ANIMAL METABOLISM.

Animals depend upon two main reactions for their energy, and for the construction of their harder tissues. The soft tissues are about the same as the plant molecules, but the hard tissues are produced by the reaction:

$$-\overset{\displaystyle H}{\underset{\displaystyle F}{\overset{|}{\underset{|}{C}}}} - \overset{\displaystyle H}{\underset{\displaystyle F}{\overset{|}{\underset{|}{C}}}} - \overset{\displaystyle H}{\underset{\displaystyle F}{\overset{|}{\underset{|}{C}}}} - + F_2 \rightarrow -\overset{\displaystyle F}{\underset{\displaystyle F}{\overset{|}{\underset{|}{C}}}} - \overset{\displaystyle F}{\underset{\displaystyle F}{\overset{|}{\underset{|}{C}}}} - \overset{\displaystyle F}{\underset{\displaystyle F}{\overset{|}{\underset{|}{C}}}} - + HF$$

resulting in a Teflon boned and shelled organism. He's going to be tough to do much with. Diatoms leave strata of powdered teflon.

The main energy reaction that occurs among this type of life is expressed in the following formula:

$$-\overset{\displaystyle H}{\underset{\displaystyle F}{\overset{|}{\underset{|}{C}}}} - \overset{\displaystyle H}{\underset{\displaystyle F}{\overset{|}{\underset{|}{C}}}} - \overset{\displaystyle H}{\underset{\displaystyle F}{\overset{|}{\underset{|}{C}}}} - \ldots + F_2 \rightarrow CF_4 + HF$$

The blood catalyst metal is titanium, which results in colorless arterial blood and violet veinous, as the titanium flips back and forth between tri- and tetravalent states.

7. SOME EFFECTS ON INTRUDING ITEMS:

Water decomposes into oxygen and hydrofluoric acid. All organic matter (earth type) converts into oxygen, carbon tetrafluoride, hydrofluoric acid, etc., with more or less speed. A rubber gas mask lasts about an hour. Glass first frosts and then disappears. Plastics act like rubber, only a little slower. The heavy metals, iron, nickel, copper, monel, etc., stand up well, forming an insoluble coat of fluorides at first and then doing nothing else.

8. WHY GO THERE?

Of great interest, naturally, are the properties of the planet which we may employ.

Large natural crystals of fluorides, such as calcium difluoride, titanium tetrafluoride, zirconium tetrafluoride, are extremely useful in optical instruments of various forms. Uranium appears as uranium hexafluoride, all ready for the diffusion process. Compounds of such non-metals as boron are obtainable from the atmosphere in high purity with very little trouble. All metallurgy must be electrical.

There are considerable deposits of beryllium, and they occur in high concentration in its ores.

—*Fletcher Pratt*

the LONG view

a novel by FLETCHER PRATT

the LONG view

a novel by FLETCHER PRATT

There was nothing to hold them together

but knowing they might be the

last people on Uller—or the first. . . .

1

THE waiter set down Greta Manning's dessert. "It's something they bring from Freya," said her father. "Called 'Dream Potion' I believe. Whatever we think of the intelligence of those psychs, I'm obliged to admit that they have elevated cookery to the status of a fine art. Good?"

"Mmmm," said Greta, allowing the pink concoction to caress her palate as she used her tongue to maneuver into a corner behind her teeth the capsule she knew she would find in it. "Too bad you don't eat sweets."

"I do not consider it a loss," said Theodore Manning, serenely. He turned to the bald-headed man. "The electronic caluculator shows that with my bodily chemistry, there is a high probability that I might lose as much as four years off my life."

The bald-headed man nodded. "Gambling is unscientific," he said, with the air of a man repeating a formula.

Greta put one hand on the table. "I think I'll go and make myself beautiful," she said, "if you don't mind waiting for a minute before we go in for the show."

Theodore Manning nodded; the bald-headed man stood up courteously. As the girl vanished through the hangings in a swirl of soft lights he sat down again and said: "Your daughter making herself beautiful impresses me as almost as unnecessary a task as proving Einstein's field theory."

Manning nodded. "Both sides of the family brought physically eugenic lines," he said. "It's the temperamental number that's dangerously high. She's a 39, even though she is a DD. As a matter of fact, that's one of the things I wanted to talk to you about before the Association went into open session. I think it's always advisable to get as many of these details settled in advance as possible, and there are certain points in the program we have worked out in the Terran Council that we would be unwilling to—expose for public discussion."

The bald-headed man said: "You can always count on the support of the Odin delegation for any truly scientific plan."

"The immediate relation of this plan to scientific advancement may not be obvious—" began Manning, and then stopped as Greta came in again, the rainbows of her party dress dancing around her. (She had read the message in the capsule and rid herself of both via the disposal chute.)

"Most perfect of fathers," she said, "your imponderable fraction of a daughter remembers that she has forgotten to tell you about something. I have a date. For after the show this evening."

"Night-spotting," said Manning. "Who is it this time?"

"Edgar Braun," she said, looking at the tablecloth. "He's found a new one. It's only twenty minutes' flight, and he says the dancers do rituals from 'way back in the twentieth century. They come from some place called Bali, where the Japanese were an imperial people. Imagine!"

Manning had a slight frown. "Isn't this the third or fourth time you've been going somewhere with this young man?" he said. "Emotional involvements are unscientific."

"Oh, pooh!" She reached over gaily and patted his cheek. "I'm as emotionally involved with him as I am with the Secretary. He just knows a lot of queer places, and we have a good time. It isn't anything like an acquaintance."

The bald-headed man, who had been glancing from one to the other, said: "Edgar Braun. That's a rather common name on Odin, where I come from. Is he from there, by any chance?"

GRETA flashed him a glance. "I think he was originally. But he came here to take his Ph.D. in vulcanology at Hawaii, because you have so few volcanoes on Odin."

The bald-headed man toyed with his spoon, and dropped it as the waiter began to collect the debris of the dinner. "Most of the Brauns tend to be moderates. There's a psych streak somewhere in the line, I've been told."

Greta laughed. "You needn't worry about Edgar. If there was a psych streak in his line, he must have come to Terra to get rid of environmental influences that could develop it. He's a perfectly good DD. I've seen his card; after all, my parent taught me that." She glanced demurely at Manning. "In fact his full number is DD-24-19. Well, in the first place, anyone with a 19 temperamental rating couldn't possibly be a psych personality, no matter how deeply the tendency might be embedded in his genes. And—" she flashed a glance at her father"—do you really think I could be interested emotionally in a 24? Ten points below me in intelligence? He'd try to repeat jokes on me to make sure I understood. In fact, he does."

Theodore Manning emitted a sigh and reached under the edge of the table to insert his thumb in the register which would automatically charge the president of the Association for the Advancement of Science with the price of the dinners. "No, I suppose not," he said. "Even the psychs tell us that women

apologize to them, then saw the bald-headed man watching her with frowning concentration, and sailed past to the place in the middle, thrusting her thumb into the socket.

The "Stellania" reached its last wonderful chords. There was a breathless pause, the screen disappeared, and they were looking into the depths of a stage that seemed to run back into infinity. A blue light lay at one corner, a yellow one at the other. No matter how often Greta had seen it, there was always a thrill in the opening of the eternal contest, and

A Strange New World

TAKE a silicone world with silicone life . . . silicone life? Why not? Life doesn't necessarily have to have our own carbon-oxygen metabolism—there are many chemical combinations possible. But given a silicone world with silicone animals and plants, Fletcher Pratt has constructed a tale in which the science is authentic and consistent and never out of character with the story. If you want an inside look at how this was done, read the author's own notes on the planet Uller which you will find elsewhere in this issue.

THE LONG VIEW, along with two companion pieces on the silicone planet, is already scheduled for book publication later in the year. Aside from its interest as a scientific exercise it also happens to be a gripping and sophisticated story which we found quite enthralling. We don't have to invite you to let us know how you like it. You will.

—*The Editor*

have a greater capacity for impersonal associative pleasure than men. What is the ancient word?—'gold-excavating'— or something like that. I think I hear the 'Stellania': shall we go in?"

The bald-headed man stood aside for Greta to take the second place, as Manning, with the assurance of a man who is bored by merely petty courtesies, and whose position has entitled him to too many of them, led the way from the dining-stall down the corridor, the yellow lightnings of his physicist's evening dress flashing around him.

The amusement room was already full, but as Manning strode down the aisle, a couple of techs next to a vacant seat scrambled out apologetically to take places farther back. Greta started to

she gripped the base of the finger-controls more firmly as out of the blue depth swam a planet, attended by twin moons. Another swam into view on the yellow side; from the lightings on them, it was evident that they were satellites of different stars. A tiny dot that would be a space-ship arced from the blue planet to one of its moons. The music took a rapid beat to indicate times and distances.

Greta, watching in frowning concentration as she made her calculations, felt the bald-headed man relax beside her with a little chuckle. He said: "I'm glad I'm here as a visitor and don't feel obligated to play. Counting the primary of that blue planet, that makes it a problem of four bodies. They don't make it that complicated for us on Odin."

She flashed him a glance. "There are a lot of techs and low-number scientists in for the Association meeting. Sssh, I want to think."

O N THE yellow planet there was a pinpoint of light, the indication to those familiar with the game that it possessed atomic explosives, and another space-ship dot soared away from it hunted vaguely through the space between and then returned to the surface. The bald-headed man said: "They're giving you plenty to work with; space travel on both of them."

From one of the moons of the blue planet, a spaceship dot rose jerkily. "Damn!" said Greta, her fingers flying. "I was afraid someone would start too soon. There hasn't been time to establish the rotational relations. There!"

The space-ship swept around in a graceful curve to the blue planet's other moon, and the girl watched intently as the bald-headed man said: "Don't you often find yourself overruled by a majority? I find it frustrating."

"Not very often," said Greta, eyes still on the stage. "This machine is set to accept the nearest accurate calculation, and the majority only controls when it's a question of calculations of the same order of accuracy. I'm pretty good at math, so I get away with quite a lot. . . ."

She broke off suddenly as two space-ships left the yellow planet in a long curve. Then: "Somebody playing on the yellow side is good; look at that, they're orbiting around each other and getting maximum mutual course correction."

She pressed keys; the music gave a skirl, and two, three, four space ships left the blue planet for its outer moon, curving in sharply. "Good girl, if you did it," chuckled the bald-headed man. "That will give greater distance capacity and better angle of approach."

Greta didn't answer; her lips a little parted, she had become utterly absorbed in the great game, as miniature space-ship after space-ship left the two planets and maneuvered toward each other in a maze more intricate than three-dimensional chess. Someone who had chosen to play on the blue side made a mistake, two of the space-ships collided and dropped back toward the planet as she said, "Damn!" again, and "We haven't an unlimited number of those." But then someone on the other side blundered, too, and one of its ships shot off at a long tangent to the very limit of the theatre, from which there came a flash to announce it was lost.

In the central space the opposing fleets were marshalling, the yellows moving the more rapidly, but also more raggedly, not seeming to have quite the precision Greta's accurate calculations were giving their opponents. They approached each other; there were little flashes here and there, and the miniature space-ships began to disappear as hits were scored. The losses were not all on one side, but the blues, with their compact formation and better maneuvering, were clearly gaining, gaining. Suddenly, the yellow fleet split apart, was decimated, in full retreat. A murmur rose from the audience as the pursuing blues swept them away—all but one, which almost unnoticed, slipped past the outskirts of the blue fleet toward its home planet.

It closed in suddenly, there was the flicker of light that meant a super-nuclear bomb, the whole planet began to burn, and abruptly the curtain was closed and the lights in the amusement room came on.

Greta, her face downcast, turned toward her father. He was sitting with his hands still on the controls, a smile that might be triumph on his countenance.

"Oh!" said the girl, "You did that! It wasn't fair!"

"The phrase is unscientific and tinged with emotionalism," said Theodore Manning. " 'Fair' is a term from the old civil courts, I believe, relating to the period before it became possible to achieve scientifically accurate results from a given combination of factors."

II

THEODORE MANNING snapped the key on the phone to the "Out; Make Record" position, adjusted the panel beside his chair to show the face of anyone at the door without showing his own and sat down.

"Do you care for tobacco?" he said; "Or a spray of some kind in the room?"

"No thanks," said the bald-headed man. "Without neglecting the amenities, we're a little more austere on Odin than the home planet, and I never acquired either habit."

"Pity," said Manning, taking out a cigar and lighting it. "You miss a good deal." He drew in a couple of reflective puffs, and then; "As a matter of fact, I'm rather glad my daughter isn't here."

A small smile was visible at the corner of the bald-headed man's mouth. "I have been wondering when the exalted President of the Association for the Advancement of Science would get around to explaining why he invited a minor delegate from Odin to dinner."

"Sarcasm does not become you," said Manning. "Nor does false modesty. As a matter of fact, here on Terra we call the Odin scientists who are disposed to cooperate with our more advanced elements the Lauria group, and leave it at that."

"I see," said Lauria, and waited.

"I suppose you have considered means of dealing with the psychs yourself."

The bald-headed man's impassiveness suddenly deserted him. "We've considered it to the point of over-production of adrenalin!" he cried. "But what can we do? We not only have them to fight, but the damned moderates! We tried to get the marriage rejection regulation repealed on Odin, just for that one planet, and do you think we could do it? I'll be damned if we could! Moderates!" He spat the word. "And they call themselves scientists!"

"I am glad you feel so strongly about it," said Manning. "The more advanced scientists here on Terra have long since reached the conclusion that the only way to break up this connection between the moderates and those confounded witch-doctors, the psychs, is to eliminate the latter from the Association entirely."

"Wouldn't the psychs appeal to the political authorities?"

Manning smiled. "That might have some weight on a few of the outer planets, where the environment is still incompletely subdued; Magni, for example, or even to a lesser degree, your own. I can assure you that on Terra or Venus or Thor, the political authorities are only a kind of game for people of low I. Q.'s—techs, or artists or servs. We merely go before them and present a scientifically established fact, and they make the necessary changes in the regulations."

"All right, then." Lauria patted himself on the top of his naked skull. "The political authorities won't interfere if you succeed in eliminating the psychs from the Association as unscientific. But how do you propose to accomplish that? They have votes in the Association, and so do the damned moderates."

"Did it ever occur to you how the votes of the psychs are cast in the parent Association?"

"No. What difference does it make?"

"It makes a good deal, as it happens. The psychs are inordinately proud of always being a unit on every question. They consider this agreement one of the proofs of the 'fact', as they call it, that psychology is really a science."

"Yes, I have heard something about that," said Lauria. "In fact, they took away the license to practice of one on Odin because he couldn't agree with the others on a diagnosis."

MANNING said: "You wander into reminiscence, which is unscientific. Therefore, when any question comes up for decision, the vote of the psychs is cast as a unit—and it is cast by the No.

1 psych, the one with the highest intelligence rating."

"Who is at present old Henrik Kool," said Lauria. "As stubborn a man as I know about. Do you suggest that the next man in line might be more amenable and that Kool is not immortal?"

"I suggest nothing of the kind. The resort to violence is barbarous, and all our advanced group would be the first to condemn it. Moreover, the next man in line is Walter Trevenna, I believe, and we should gain nothing by substituting him for Kool. No. We have developed a far better and more subtle plan."

"Go ahead."

"What would you say if I told you that I know of a psych with an 11 intelligence rating?"

Lauria's eyes opened wide. "I would first say that you were perpetrating a joke and then, if convinced you are serious, that I'm surprised he hasn't already been made No. 1 psych. Why, you're only a 16 yourself!"

Manning smiled again. "It's no joke, and it's perfectly extraordinary that a man with one of the lowest intelligence figures ever reached should be a psych. Or perhaps, I shouldn't call him a man yet. He's not even thirty years old, and hasn't been declared adult. The name is Lajos Harkavy—I believe Hungarian by ancestry—and his full rating is BC-11-71. Quite aside from the fact that his temperamental figure is so high that he couldn't be anything but a psych, he's interested in painting." He gave a note of utter contempt to the last word, and stopped, but as Lauria continued to look at him without saying anything, went on:

"Well, our proposal is simply to have him declared adult."

Now Lauria frowned. "I don't see . . ." he began, and then; "Let me ask two questions: how would having a man with that degree of intelligence at the head of the psych interest help our position? And how do you expect the Association to declare so young a man

adult? Is that why you want my help?"

Manning said; "That's three questions and not two, as a matter of scientific accuracy. I'll take up the first one first. Lajos Harkavy has received general scientific and special psychological training, but as I was just remarking, he seems to have a temperamental feeling for the arts. That is, if he were head of the psychs, one of two things could be expected. Either any unified action on their part would be paralyzed by internal conflicts among them, or he would remain perfectly indifferent to what happened to the general body. As a matter of fact, I believe it would not be too difficult to get him to go to Freya, where the atmosphere would take care of it that he enjoyed himself harmlessly without ever bothering us again. And as he has a good 120 years expectation of life yet, that would guarantee us a free hand for this length of time. I think it is not beyond possibility that we could get the regulations altered in a satisfactory manner; even eject the psychs altogether from the Association."

LAURIA nodded. "Your line of reasoning is convincing," he said "And I withdraw my third question. I'll be glad to help in any way I can. But the other one is still more serious; how do you propose to have him declared adult?"

"There is one case in which any member of the Association can be declared adult and admitted to full participation, provided he has a low-number intelligence rating. That is—when he marries."

"I see. So you propose to set up an acquaintance looking toward marriage for this Harkavy. Did you have anyone special in mind?"

Manning laid down his cigar. "I have. My daughter, Greta Manning."

Lauria made a sound which could not be interpreted in words.

"Divorce your mind from emotionalism," said Manning, "and consider the matter rationally. In the first place, the psychs will hardly object to the idea of their future leader marrying my daughter. The objections, if any, would come from our advanced group, and it is precisely for this reason that I asked you to drop in tonight—to tell you that the idea has my entire approval. In the second place, their intelligence numbers are within three points of each other, which makes it a eugenically desirable permanent union."

"But—" began Lauria.

Manning raised a hand. "In science, we must learn to reject merely emotional appeals; that is the thing that distinguishes us from the psychs. I am quite aware that she is my daughter, and I have the normal paternal feelings toward her. However, as we were remarking earlier, her temperamental number is dangerously low, and I have reason to believe that she has been contacting some of the moderates, perhaps is involved with them. We managed to get a spy ray on Toijiru Shigemitsu, and it reported she had met him at least once."

"You overwhelm any objections I can make before I think of them," said Lauria, "but I still have one more. How do you know the acquaintance will result in a marriage? That is, may not this Harkavy already have an emotional involvement?"

"It doesn't matter. People with anywhere near as low an intelligence number as his are excessively rare, and if either she or Harkavy should reject the acquaintance, they might be forced to take it up again at the age of compulsory marriage. As for any emotional involvement Harkavy has at present, it may be dismissed; his intelligence rating is so high that he could not conceivably be allowed to marry any such person. For that matter, I don't think he has much opportunity where he is; he's out on Uller."

"That's one of the aberrant planets, isn't it? Silicone chemistry as I remember, and just barely habitable."

"That's right. Why anyone should want to go there, I can't imagine, but he seems to consider it a good place to practice his art."

Lauria said; "Very well, you can count on my support when the matter of the acquaintance comes up before the Eugenic Committee. I presume you yourself will have to offer objections simply for the sake of appearances?"

III

"ALL ready for a big evening?" said Edgar Braun lightly, as the serv closed the door of the flyer behind them.

"Mmm-hm," said Greta. "I'm glad you picked an evening suit with brown radiations; it will go nicely with my rainbows."

"I keep telling you we're temperamentally made for each other," he said, throwing in the switch. "If you'll only let me apply for an acquaintance—"

The little machine soared, ducked lightly to the left in response to the warning signal indicating an incoming rocket express, and steadied toward the north.

"Have you ever thought of the potentialities of model numbers?" asked Greta.

"Oh, listen, Gree—"

"You listen. I've told you a dozen times that I refuse even to think about marriage or getting emotionally involved until this thing is decided, one way or another. Besides, if we lose, there won't be any chance for emotion. The advanced group is getting awfully close to putting through that regulation about not being able to refuse any marriage recommended by the Eugenic Committee. Father's stopped talking about it, and that means he's about ready to act. Where's the meeting going to be held tonight?"

"At a casino on the shore of Lake George. Paul found a spy ray planted in the Rodman place. As a matter of fact . . ." His voice trailed off.

"As a matter of fact, what?"

"Nothing. You'll find out when you see Toijiru."

It was dark inside the flyer as the silver ribbon of the Hudson grew small beneath the moon and a Montreal-New York carrier flashed above them in the opposite direction, its port-lights gleaming like a string of fireflies. Edgar Braun swung the flyer expertly into the long slant. "Take a look back, will you?" he said. "Just to check on whether we have a tail."

Greta swung the basket-seat around and craned her neck. "Not unless he's beneath us," she said. "Who else is coming tonight?"

"Just Toijiru and Paul Frasser. It's a special; something came up. All right, close down, I'm going in."

The flyer slid down the slope, bounced once on the surface of the lake in a cloud of spray, and rounded to the pier, where a serv hooked it in and swung back the door. As they climbed out the lights from the casino windows caught Greta's dress and once more turned it to a garment of rainbows, while the soft beat of music came from within.

"This is a queer place to hold a meeting," said Greta. "Are you sure that the spray and the drinks won't affect our thinking?"

"Toijiru thought of that. There are some little summerhouses on the hill at the back, and after you and I have had a dance or two, we're to go out there and meet them. I have the directions."

The outer door slid back as he placed his hands in the black-light ray, and they were in the corridor, being greeted by a bowing superior serv, who bowed still more deeply at the full unit Braun slid into his hand, and led the way to the inner door.

A FINE wave of spray met them with a pulse-tingling effect at the door; a dance had just ended, and exotically-clad couples were laughing and talking as they made their way back to the tables. As the serv led them to one,

Braun said; "I don't suppose you have any idea of what your father is planning for the Association meeting?"

"Sssh," said Greta, "you never can tell who might overhear." Then as they sat down; "Not precisely, only it's going to be something pretty tricky. He had dinner with the head delegate from Odin tonight, and yesterday it was one from Venus, and they both belong to the advanced group already."

"I don't see how—" said Braun, and paused to give an order to the waiter, then completed his remark, "—how that makes any difference."

"Don't you? They'd vote for anything he proposed. He must be getting them ready to vote for something he doesn't propose."

"I wouldn't have thought of that."

"I know, Ed. That's one of the reasons I won't accept an acquaintance with you."

The orchestra swung into a smooth rhythm that had its origin on one of the outer planets, and Edgar Braun, his face a little stricken, stood up and offered her his hand. The spray, as usual, was intensifying his emotions. As she pillowed her head against his shoulder, Greta said; "Just this one. It's a long dance, and I think we can slip out when it ends. Come on, play up and pretend you're deliriously happy with me."

He swung her through the movement of the dance, then they paused for a moment, making a pretense of consultation before he led her toward the exit at the back. There were gravel paths beyond the outer door here, winding up the slope among the trees, with muted lights set close to the ground to prevent stumbling. "Put your arm around me," commanded Greta, as they passed a turn-off that led to one of the summer-houses. "We have to make it look good, even if we don't feel that way."

"But I do," said Braun. "That's just the trouble. Here's the one, I think."

He swung her round the curve past a screen of bushes and up to the summer-

"Come out of it!" Greta commanded

house. A light flashed dazzlingly in their faces, then shut off abruptly, and Paul Frasser's voice said; "It's all right. We're here."

The little kiosk was intended for only two people, and the four of them had to squeeze close into the seat. Somebody touched the transparent weather-shielding into position, and Toijiru Shigem-

itsu's voice said out of the dark; "This is a very special meeting, particularly for you, Greta. They're getting ready to move."

"I know that already," said the girl.

"You don't know all of it. Your father is going to have an order of acquaintance put through the Eugenic Committee for you."

There was a momentary silence. Then Greta said, low and hard; "I won't accept. I'll reject the acquaintance even before it starts."

"You had better hear the rest of it," said Shigemitsu. "He isn't going to offer it himself; in fact, I wouldn't be surprised if he pretended to object. The acquaintance is one he could object to— Lajos Harkavy, who's going to be leader of the psychs as soon as he is declared adult."

They couldn't see her mouth work in the dark, but it was a minute or two before she answered. "I've heard of him. Isn't he—?"

Shigemitsu said; "He has one of the best intelligence numbers ever recorded, lower even than yours. The Eugenics Committee will put on every bit of pressure it can to bring the acquaintance to a marriage."

IN THE dark someone who must have been Edgar Braun touched and squeezed the girl's hand as Shigemitsu paused and then went on: "The trouble is that Harkavy's temperamental rating is bad—"

"I thought that one of the reasons I was working with you people was to do away with all that."

"Let me go on. I use the word 'bad' only in the sense that the advanced group use it. Harkavy has psych training, but he appears to be more interested in painting, and Paul's contacts say that he's pretty lazy, just about the type the advanced group would want to use as a stooge. With him at the head of the psychs, they might be able to get through any number of new regulations —even the one they've been trying for to make all marriages compulsory."

Paul Frasser's deep voice added; "They might even make their own group into a kind of sacred priesthood; without the psych vote, we're outnumbered badly in the Association."

Greta said; "They're a priesthood already, a grinding priesthood that has already wiped out nearly every bit of personal liberty in the worlds. Why, think, if—"

Shigemitsu said; "Yes. But we haven't much time."

"All right, then," said Greta. "The practical question; what do you want me to do?"

"Accept the acquaintance. We haven't any grounds for protesting it now before the Eugenic Committee or in the Association, and we don't understand what's going on. Perhaps your father suspects you of working with the moderates, or perhaps it's only that he wants to bring the psychs to his support somehow. Find out what this Harkavy chap is like and what he intends to do. Find out what his connection with your father's group is. Plant a spy-ray on him if you can."

Greta shivered a little in the dark, although it was very warm with the four of them in the restricted summer-house. "You remember what we were talking about? What if my father's group succeeds in getting through the regulation making marriages compulsory after an acquaintance has been accepted? And I'm stuck for the rest of my life with this—this—"

Shigemitsu said quietly; "I have two sons. One of them had scientific status, and went to Venus. He didn't like what was happening in the swamp-mines there, and he couldn't get anyone interested, so he tried to organize some of the servs themselves in protest. They tried him for trying to elevate civil authority over scientific, reduced him to a tech, and sent him to Freya. He's still there, oh, quite happy when we hear from him—breathing in that Freya atmosphere and unable to do his own thinking. He will probably live another hundred years, but we count him as already dead."

Greta shivered again and rustled upright. "All right. I see what you mean. Only it's a little hard to take a chance on mortgaging your whole life just to find out something that ought to be easy to find out, anyway."

Braun held the door open for her, then followed her out onto the path. The sound of footsteps came from somewhere up the slope, and she said; "— lovely, but I do want one more drink before we go home."

"You're entitled to one more at least," he said aloud, then under his breath and with his head close to hers; "Gree! There's one way you can get out of this acquaintance, and not have anyone object. You can take up a non-marriage connection with me. Will you?"

"No, Edgar." She put a hand on his arm. "I wouldn't be in this at all if I didn't believe that everyone should be allowed to live his own life, without scientists or anyone else telling them what to do. To do what you suggest would be choosing compulsion to avoid another."

Behind them in the dark Paul Frasser said to Shigemitsu; "She is very young. One might almost think that she really considered emotional decisions as having value. Are you not afraid that this Harkavy will convert her fully to the psych position? It would be a pity to lose our best spy in the advanced group."

"I don't think you need to be concerned," said Shigemitsu. "If we lose our spy in the advanced group, we gain one with the psychs. She can hardly refuse to continue working with us in view of what we could make known of her past activities. A charge of betrayal of trust is quite as serious as one of inciting social unrest to the advantage of the civil authorities."

IV

WHEN the annunciator sounded, Greta was deep in the Diophantine analysis of a second-order Riemann equation. She sighed, put down her calculator, shot the results thus far attained into a recorder, and pressed the button. The face that looked from the box was that of a stranger; young, thin and straight, with lines of humor showing around the mouth.

"Miss Manning?" it said.

"Yes."

"I am Lajos Harkavy. May I see you for a few minutes?"

"Why—I thought you were on Uller."

"I was. That's one of the things I want to see you about."

Her face became ever so slightly frigid. "I don't know—"

"Surely you can spare me a few minutes—under the circumstances. I'll even promise to be entertaining."

"All right. It's the 3 button, 42nd story."

She frowned as she switched the connection off, touched the inter-room communicator and made sure her father wasn't home, and almost as a reflex gesture, checked her eye-shadow before the entrance-wall slid back. He was taller than she expected, and wearing an inflatable as though he had just come from a space-liner.

"Won't you come in?" she said, indicating a chair.

"Thank you." He waited for her to sit down before taking his own place, and it occurred to her that was exactly what an irrational psych would do, expecting her to be impressed by the antique minor courtesy. "I understand we have been named for an acquaintance," he said.

"The Eugenics Committee passed it this morning. How did you find out so quickly?"

Lajos Harkavy smiled. "Not very difficult. Even out on our little paradise on Uller there are copies of the priority lists, and it wasn't hard to guess that with our respective ratings, they'd at least make a try at bringing us together. What I want you to do is reject the acquaintance."

Greta felt a totally irrational anger at being asked to do what she had herself intended to do. "Indeed!" she said. "May I ask why you don't reject it yourself?"

"You may. And I'll answer that it's for reasons personal to me, which won't seem logical to you as an advanced scientist, but it will have to do for the moment. I want to present you with the reasons why you should reject in your own interest."

"And what are they?"

He looked around the room. "I notice you haven't any room-spray on, and not a single picture in the place. You wouldn't like the way I live. I like sprays, I like fun—and I paint pictures." This last was uttered with subtle overtones of defiance.

"That might turn out to be the basis of an incompatibility making a rejection of marriage necessary after the acquaintance period. It isn't one for rejecting the acquaintance."

He grinned. "All right, you're an advanced scientist, and I'm what you would call a psych, with a poor temperament rating. I find pure mathematics, or pure science of any kind, an unholy bore. What could we say to each other, or do together, during an acquaintance?"

Greta said; "That's what you said before, only you're putting it in other words. It's an ingenious device in dialectics, but you'll have to do better. And besides, my own temperament rating is 39; I could just as easily be a moderate. You're making assumptions."

HE GRINNED sardonically. "And you're trying to change the ground of the discussion. I'm onto that one. Let's see—why else should you refuse the acquaintance? For one thing, I'm living on Uller, at least until I finish the series of paintings I'm working on. You wouldn't like it there."

"You don't have to tell me. I looked it up when this acquaintance warrant came through. The weather is terrible, the water tastes like soap and has to be distilled, the animals are foul, and you have to use an artificial day-night routine. That only answers your last objection. There would be plenty we could do together, mostly on the adventure side."

"What ambition!" said Lajos, and stretched his legs lazily. "And what an ambition! But don't think you'll get me into anything like that. I prefer air-conditioned rooms with a slight spray in them, and the only adventure I'm interested in is the kind that concerns—females."

"And yet you want one to refuse an acquaintance! I'm still waiting to hear why I should."

For answer, Lajos got up and paced slowly across the floor, then back again. Then he came over to Greta's chair and in a new voice, quite low, said; "Is there any chance of a spy-ray around this place?"

"I don't think so, but—"

"No. I don't dare risk it. But believe me, there's a very good reason, not connected with myself at all—"

Greta stood up. "Now you've made me curious. I suppose that, being a psych, you deliberately applied the stimuli to bring it about, but you succeeded. There's a park just across the river on the old Palisades. Let's go look at nature."

He didn't say anything more as she dialled for the duty serv to bring the runabout to the terrace, or when they got in and soared away across the stream, and she was well enough aware of the possibility of a spy-ray being planted in the machine not to say anything either.

The park was bright and green in the fresh spring air; Greta parked the runabout at the entrance and they strolled down a walk between a double row of monstrous blue lilies from one of the outer planets, to a bench.

Greta seated herself and said; "Now will you tell me about it?"

He frowned. "All right, I will. It's just this: if you follow me to Uller on an acquaintance, there's a good chance you may never be able to get back."

"Why not?"

"Your father hasn't told you? About the shortages? And the reason why the production committee has been moved to Venus? Didn't he tell you?"

She shook her head. "Not a word."

"It's a pretty carefully guarded secret. But the essence of it is that there's a major shortage of beryllium, and it's system-wide."

"For moderators in power plants and ship drives? Why can't they use the old-style carbon moderators? They still do in some places."

"On planets. You forget that when you use a carbon moderator in the double reaction for interstellar drive, it's so inefficient that it doubles the consumption of fissionables. The system has enough uranium to hike along for quite a while yet on normal consumption rates, what with the discovery of an occasional new planet that can be worked for uranium, but if you double everything up, we'll soon be in the position they were here on Terra when the oil reserves began to run out."

Greta said; "That is, things slowing up everywhere, and revolutions, and—"

"Not quite as bad as that. There are plenty of power sources and plenty of uranium to keep the planets running individually, and even for interplanetary travel, where there are two habitable planets in the same system, and they only use the primary reaction drive. But interstellar travel is going to go right out the window, and soon. That is, unless something happens."

"So that's why—" began Greta, and flushed.

"Why what?" said Lajos.

"I was just going to say that must be the reason for that regulation last year —the one restricting interstellar travel to people with scientific status and requiring an authorization from a local board."

"I daresay that's part of it. But it seemed to me that you were going to say something else."

"You psychs are too clever by forty per cent." The girl's voice had an edge

[*Turn page*]

to it. "Thank you for the information—and for your solicitude about my welfare. Now I'll give you a piece of information, too. I never had any attention of accepting an acquaintance with you, and I wouldn't accept one with a man who paints, even if he had an intelligence rating of point one. Does that answer your question?"

TO HER surprise, Harkavy merely rose from the bench, and stood frowning. He was very tall, she observed. "No," he said, "it doesn't. Not at all. I don't understand why a member of the advanced group, who would be left in control of practically everything if interstellar travel were cut off, and could sit in their corners doing mathematical puzzles all day while everyone else worked for them, should develop so much heat over the prospect."

"You don't have to—" she began, but before she could say any more two figures in the decent blue uniforms of Regulator Techs turned the corner of the path and came straight toward them. One of them stepped up to the young man.

"You are Lajos Harkavy?" he said.

"Yes."

"Please come with us. The charge is making an unauthorized interstellar voyage, contrary to regulations."

Greta clutched the arm of one of the Regulators. "What are you going to do to him?"

The man shrugged. "It's a major regulation. Probably they'll deport to Freya as temperamentally unstable. That's the usual line."

"But you can't do that!"

"I'm not doing it," said the Regulator. "If you've got a song and dance, give it to the Rating Committee."

Greta said; "You can't do it, and I'll tell you why. We both have scientific status, and this is the first day of an accepted acquaintance. I think the order of the Eugenics Committee takes precedence over any violation of regulations except acts of violence. And I

don't want to go to Freya."

"It sure does, lady," said the Regulator, stepping back, and turning to his companion; "Get your phone out and check that, will you, Morgan?"

V

GRETA stood looking out the window toward where the depressing landscape of Uller stretched under brown, rubbery grasses to the shore of the slick-looking Matteran Sea. A lorcha was coming in from the Cape Holland fishing station, the deck-hand swinging his arms to keep warm, as he waited for the craft to slide in to the gate of the processing plant where he could hook in the automatic draw.

The girl said; "The spy-ray was a mistake. He waited until he said goodnight, then handed me the disc and said, 'By the way, here's your plaything. I like to keep a certain amount of privacy.' I suppose I had it coming."

Paul Frasser did not stir from his seat. "A man with his intelligence is hard to handle. But I'm beginning to wonder if the whole operation wasn't a mistake. From what I can make out, there's nothing in him we can use. All he's interested in is painting and night-spots."

Outside the sun rim met the horizon redly, and the day wind that had ruffled the surface of the sea to long undulant swells was falling. Greta turned, the edges of her hair redly outlined by the light.

"There's something—almost mysterious in him," she said. "And after all, he did find out about the beryllium shortage."

Frasser grunted. "That could have happened in a number of ways. After all, he's going to be titular leader of the psychs some day. Maybe someone in your father's group thought it would be a good idea to let him know. What does he say about it, by the way?"

"That it's a problem for applied

scientists, and he isn't interested."

"That's what I told you, Gree. People who put a wall of mystery around themselves generally haven't much behind it except a desire to amuse themselves, and I will say that Harkavy is devoting himself to that with all the resources of his high-power intelligence. Calling him mysterious is just a relic of the pre-scientific age. What's mysterious about him?"

"Well—he won't even sleep at my quarters.

"Is that surprising? Probably has someone coming to his. It wouldn't be the first time it had happened on Uller. Better break the acquaintance. We have work to do."

The sun was half way below the horizon now, and the lights were beginning to stream automatically from walls and ceiling in compensation. Greta Manning shook her head:

"No, Paul. The job of trying to make it a world, a universe, where everyone gets a square deal whether they have a high eugenic number or not, means everything in the world to me. You know that. That's why I accepted this acquaintance in the first place, when I didn't want to a bit. But I've accepted it now and given my word, and so has Lajos; and I won't pull out and I won't cheat, either."

Frasser snorted. "Emotionalism! Unscientific—"

"Isn't it just to give everybody a chance at unscientific emotionalism that we're doing what we are, Paul? To keep people from being bred like animals for the production of more pure scientists? There are already too many."

Frasser said; "That sounds odd, coming from—oh, well, let's not quarrel. We're in this together, and up to our necks."

"Yes, aren't we, though!" She was cheerful again in a second. "What time is it? I've got to go. I promised Malya Bryussov I'd come over and look at the new method of calculating high primes she thinks she's found, but I don't believe it's anything more than Lucas and a calculating machine."

THE air-lock at the door hissed slightly as she ran out. Frasser sat in frowning silence for a moment, then got up and put on his heated garments; no matter how long he stayed on Uller, he could not find himself comfortable at a temperature of 7° C. His quarters were on 2nd Street, which meant he had only a brief walk past the buildings of fused sandstone, built squat and monolithic to withstand the hurricane winds of Uller, before reaching the square, with its pylon-like beam tower in the center and the Communications Center on the other side.

Work had just closed down for the day, and in the hall inside people were tapping their communication-boxes for letters and the reels of the day's news. Frasser nodded to one or two, pretended not to notice a superior tech who was coming toward him and would either want a promotion or the endorsement of an authorization for an interstellar flight, and went down the broad staircase that led to the long-range communications room.

"I want a tight-beam communication to Terra," he said to the clerk behind the desk. "To Toijiru Shigemitsu, DD-32-28, New York, Terra."

The clerk started to punch in the numbers, then looked up. "Pardon me, sir, but are you a scientist? There's a new reg—"

"What the hell would I be asking for an interstellar tight beam for if I wasn't?" demanded Frasser. He fished in a pocket, produced the metal identifier, flung it on the counter, and viciously punched his thumb down on the checking machine. "What's your name and number? You deserve a report for disrespect."

The clerk's lip trembled slightly. "Ector Mariscal, sir, RB-122-18. I'm sorry, sir, but I hadn't seen you before."

"All right," said Frasser. "I'll drop it. When will you have the beam set up?"

"I don't know, sir. They're having a little trouble at Station No. 6—a gonflar got in and damaged the tower—and Terra may be on that side. But I'll put an urgent on it. Do you want me to call you at your quarters, or will you take it here?"

"Might as well wait. I haven't anything else to do."

"Will you take the fourth compartment, sir? You know where the reels are?"

Frasser nodded, initialed the five-unit chit the clerk shoved at him, and pushed down the hall to the compartment marked "4," where it occurred to him to have any incoming calls at his quarters transferred to the Center. A light spray would do him good, he decided, so he turned one on, and then settled himself to contemplate the reels of the day's news. There was a picture of the gonflar being driven from Station 6, one after another of its six legs developing an odd hurrying motion as the stimulus-whip was applied to that section by armored guards; a mentally unstable tech who had murdered his wife was telling his tale to a psych; and then a woman with a long face began to explain how much she would do if elected—and Frasser turned the machine off.

FROM the speaker in the wall a voice said abruptly; "Your connection, sir," and Shigemitsu's voice followed, slightly blurred by crossing light years of space; "Toijiru Shigemitsu here."

"Watakushi-wa uta-wo kiki-tai," said Frasser.

"Sora wa umai," came the answer. "I think we may omit the remainder of the challenge and response, my friend. I recognize your voice. Why do you call?"

"She's getting balky. Resisted the suggestion that she break off the acquaintance before it ran its full term."

Shigemitsu said; "Have you considered that he may have decided that it would be useful to turn the connection into a marriage, and is applying his knowledge of psychology to her?"

"Bah! It's just those romantic ideas we noticed before she left. She talks about having given her word, and that sort of thing."

"You don't think she's really attracted to him?"

"Only to the biological function extent. Otherwise, he's about as useless a piece of furniture as I've ever seen."

"Still, it might be useful to have him at the head of the psychs and her in our interest."

"He's going to refuse the appointment and turn artist. At least that's what she thinks. And she's too valuable a piece of property for our side to be wasted like that."

"I see." Shigemitsu was silent for two ticks. Then: "The other matter?"

"You mean Rizzi? I don't think we can bring him over. I talked to him for a couple of hours. He agreed that there was a strong possibility that Niflheim was extremely rich in beryllium, just as you deduced from the registers. Also that there would be a big promotion waiting for anyone who could find a way to get at it through that fluorine atmosphere. But in the first place, he didn't think it could be done, and in the second, he didn't seem interested. Wants things to go on the way they are. After all, he's an 18, which would make him pretty close to No. One man out here if all interstellar travel were cut off. He's an applied scientist, sure, but there aren't more than two or three pures on the planet."

"Did you try putting the girl on him?"

"Yes, and ran into more romantic ideas. She said that she wouldn't cheat while conducting an acquaintance with Harkavy."

"My friend," said Shigemitsu, "you are insufficiently subtle. It is a quality of race, which has nothing to do with intelligence. I think I perceive the answer to our problem. You are keeping a careful check on Harkavy's movements?"

"As close as I can. The spy-ray failed;

he found it where she planted it and gave her back the disc, so I had to go back to primitive methods and have him personally followed. So far the reports have been devoid of interest."

EVEN over the long-range beam, Frasser could hear the slight hissing sound with which Shigemitsu habitually began one of his trap-questions. "What do the reports concern?" he asked.

"Matters like this; subject spent the afternoon in a glassine hut on Cape Lion, painting a view of the Matteran Sea. Subject spent the evening having dinner with his acquaintance, took her to her quarters after a session in the game-room, and then spent a good part of the night at the Cave of the Four Winds night-club in the company of a lady who calls herself Roselle La Blanche, and who makes a profession of exhibiting her torso—"

"One moment."

"Yes?" said Frasser.

"You have the key to the situation in your hands. How often do these night-club visits take place?"

"Frequently."

"And you have just told me that the girl will not, as you put it, 'cheat' while conducting an acquaintance with Harkavy? Does it not occur to you that she would take an unreasonably romanticized attitude toward his connection with this ecdysiast?"

"I never thought of such a thing."

"Begin thinking of it." Shigemitsu was crisp. "You are dealing with a person who lacks the normal scientific objectivity, a temperamental 39. Arrange to take her to this night-club when the two of them are there together. You will not need to apply any other pressures."

VI

HER VOICE apologetic, Greta said; "I'm sorry I couldn't make it last night. But I was working on a new postulated geometry that turned out to be perfectly logical at speeds in excess of n prime. The beauty of it is that it's perfectly useless; there aren't any speeds in excess of n prime."

Frasser gazed at her a moment. "I sometimes wonder if that isn't the trouble," he said. "You people in the pure sciences have precedence over everyone else, but the only time you're happy is when your work is useless. And now the machine is running down. Are you going to wear that?"

Greta glanced down at her costume, which was being touched to multi-colored flames as it caught the lights from walls and ceiling. "My rainbow dress? Why not? It's a party."

"It's unusual for the guests to wear luminant clothes in the place we're going. It's a little on the rough side, and they're apt to be taken for—well, professionals."

"Oh." She considered. "I don't suppose it would hurt me to be propositioned, but you're probably right. Wait a minute." She disappeared into the back and presently returned in a dress which, while still definitely for the evening, gave off only soft tones of green. Paul Frasser tried the communication box, found it locked, and was gazing at the ceiling when she came back. "I have the flier on the roof," he said. "It didn't seem worth while bringing it in for the time I'd wait for you."

He stepped ahead of her to the elevator. "Where is this place?" she asked as they emerged on the shadowy roof, shivering slightly at the impact of the chill Uller night.

"Way out past the cape. Most of the habitues come from the tide-control project; techs and servs, and a fairly hard gang at that."

The flier took off smoothly, bucked once, and straightened out on course. Far below and to the right there was a blaze of brilliance around New Ravenna's interstellar port, and conveying machines were waddling clumsily up to deposit their burdens in the huge bulk of an interstellar freighter.

"They're pushing it hard on liquid silicones from the fisheries," remarked Frasser. "Trying to stock-pile lubricants against the date when there won't be any interstellar travel."

Greta shuddered slightly beside him. "But what's going to happen to all those people?" she asked. "The techs and servs who have been brought in here to do the work on the promise of more money and quick home leaves?"

"They'll have to stay on Uller, that's all. But I think sympathy for them is wasted. They're not first-class minds and the resources of this place are sufficient to provide everything they really need. What gets me down is that your father's precious advanced group is quite ready to put applied scientists in the same category. Getting the warning about the beryllium shortage is one thing we can thank you for."

"Have you been in touch with Shigemitsu?" asked the girl. "Is he going to do anything in the Association Council?"

"I doubt if he'll try to do anything immediately. If he would make the information about the shortage public, it would not only stir up the techs and servs, but the applied scientists would be charged with the responsibility for not having foreseen and provided against the shortage, and as a result, our moderate group would be just about blown apart."

"If we could only . . ." began Greta; then, "There's the Cape."

"I have it on the screen. Button up, we're going in." He worked controls. Below them, the contours of the formless black mass of the night club building were picked out by infra-red in the moonless night of Uller in answer to his landing beam, and as the flier slid in, servs hooded against the cold came running out to guide it to the ramp of the underground hangar.

The door cut off the stars behind; Paul Frasser handed Greta out, accepted the offered check and steered her toward the elevator, where a bored serv slowly returned to his pocket a reel and the eye-piece through which he had been contemplating it.

THE first thing of which Greta became conscious when they reached the level of the club itself was a quantity of spray in the air that almost made her head swim; the next was that the place was circular, and in accordance with its name, was decorated to resemble some huge, rock-hewn cave back in Terra. There was no dancing at the moment; the decorative scheme had been carried into the permanent music, which was that of winds howling through an aeolian harp. The lights were dim; she had reached their table before she could see enough of her surroundings to make out that Paul Frasser had not exaggerated about the character of the place. Most of those present were clearly techs and servs, some still in their working garments, accompanied by shrill-voiced girls to whom the low level of the lighting was a charity.

Frasser ordered drinks and looked around. "Well, what do you think of low life?" he asked. "Some of the dancing is really remarkable, though."

The spray was having its effect; she felt a thrill of adventure tingle up and down her spine. "Do they have fights?"

"If they do, they're stopped pretty quickly. Do you see those two techs at that third table? They're Regulators. Hello, there's Derek Hyde!" He half stood and waved to a man sitting alone at a table across the room, who got up and sauntered over, bringing his drink.

There were introductions; Derek Hyde accepted an invitation to join the couple, and it was explained to him that Miss Manning had come for the dancing.

"Good idea," said Hyde. "It's better in a place like this than in the regular establishments. More emotional and unrestrained. They have one girl here who would be wonderful anywhere in the system. Her name's Roselle La Blanche, and I think she comes from Venus; how she drifted here, I haven't any idea. Just about due, too."

The music became one of the quick double-steps from the inner planets and couples covered the floor Greta said: "Where do the women come from?"

"Most of them are servs from New Ravenna," said Frasser. "They have to have an ostensible profession, you know."

The music stopped, but instead of taking up its windy background rhythm again, swung into a quicker pace that changed and rose to a pitch of the most intense emotion. Then, suddenly, all the lights went out, to flash back on as abruptly, showing a girl standing alone in the center of the floor.

"That's her, now," said Derek Hyde. There was no doubt that she was somebody, and fully conscious of it, as she caught up the beat, and with a slow, seductive movement, began to weave through a figure, the strings of opals in which she seemed to be entirely clothed picking up the light from floor, wall, ceiling, in a thousand shifting patterns. One of the opal-chains came loose and slithered across the floor as she moved; then another, and another, as the men in the audience began to shout and stamp, until finally, in a sudden whirl of motion, she lost the last chain of opals just as the helmet of dark hair broke from her head to cover her nearly to the knees and the lights were extinguished for a second time.

"You were right," said Gret, "that was wonderful."

"So is she," said Paul Frasser. "I wouldn't mind knowing her myself. In fact—"

Derek Hyde turned toward him. "It's no use, old man. She's already got a connection—with that high number psych out here. You know, the crazy one, that's turning down his scientific rating to be an artist. Harkvaly, or something like that."

[Turn page]

A S THE emotion-intensifying spray touched her, it set Greta's fingers to gripping the table so hard they hurt. In a quick intense voice, she said: "Do you mean Lajos Harkavy?"

"Yes, that's the one. Why?"

Frasser said: "Miss Manning is here on acquaintance with him."

"Oh, look here," said Hyde, "I'm sorry. I didn't mean—"

"Paul," said Greta, "get the superior serv. I want to talk to her at once. I don't care what it costs. Use my rank. I want to talk to her. I have to talk to her."

Around them the music had risen again and couples were dancing. As Frasser beckoned for the serv, Greta's hand went out in an impulsive gesture and tipped over her drink, but it sank at once into the absorbent table.

Derek Hyde said again, "I'm really sorry—"

"It doesn't matter," said the girl. "Please go away."

Paul Frasser said, "Really, Greta, I had no idea—"

"It doesn't matter, I tell you. I want to talk to her."

Roselle La Blanche came down between the tables behind the superior serv. Her hair had been hastily gathered up, and she had thrown something around her; the techs whistled at her as she passed, and one or two of them tried to pinch her.

The superior serv said, "This is Miss Manning. She's a high-ranking pure scientist and wanted to talk to you."

Roselle La Blanche slid into the place vacated by Derek Hyde. "To me?" she said. "Why, certainly, honey, though I don't know what about. I don't know about anything that would be good for a pure scientist." She giggled a little.

Greta said, "About just one thing. Do you have a connection with Lajos Harkavy?"

The beautiful, slightly vapid face of the dancer hardened. "I don't know that it's any of your business."

"Tell me!"

"You're being emotional. Honey, they always told me that people with scientific rating were rational. I was going to ask you for a unit and a half for bringing me out here, but I'll give it to you for free. You oughta take a treatment." She stood up, flashed a come-on smile at Frasser, and was gone.

For a minute Greta didn't say anything. Then, with both hands on the table, she said, "Paul, have you a message going soon?"

"Yes. It's technical."

"Make it partly personal. Tell Edgar Braun I'm coming back to him as soon as the next ship leaves. And take me back to my quarters."

At the elevator, he checked suddenly. "Dammit," he said, "wait for me. I forgot to leave anything for the serv."

But it was not the serv he hurried back into the club to speak to; it was Derek Hyde, and he said, "Here. You did a wonderful job. It worked out just right."

"I'LL GO with you because I promised," said Greta. "But you might as well know now that I'm going to refuse the marriage." Her voice was flat.

Lajos Harkavy stopped tightening the strap on his portable easel. "Any particular reason?" he asked.

She felt herself flushing and half-turned her head. "No. Just the general one that we don't seem temperamentally suited to each other."

"I would have said quite the opposite. In fact, you make me wonder, frankly, whether some ulterior factor has not developed that—"

"Oh, you and your psychology!" She stamped her foot, and then suddenly flashed into a smile. "There's no use quarrelling about it though, now. Let's have as good a time as we can out of what's left. Where are we going?"

"To a place about eight hundred miles north of here—MacMurray Forest. Ever hear of it?"

"Didn't some of your pictures come from there?"

He slung the easel and box of paints on his back. "Yes, but not at this time of year. The colors are really spectacular when the leaves begin to come out, and I want to try to catch them with luminescents that will give the effect of changing light. Got the food package?"

He pushed the button for the wall slide, then clicked the communicator. "Harkavy. Will you send my flier up? and drop a report on wind conditions at seventeen degrees north, MacMurray Forest area on the seat."

The sun was just coming up to the southeast as they stepped out of the elevator head onto the wind-blown roof and the sky was streaked from south to north with long fingers of dun-colored cloud, red along their lower edges. Greta glanced at them and said, "Could you catch something like that with your luminescents?"

He shook his head. "I could probably, but it's too opaque to produce an emotional reaction. That would only be representational painting."

"But how do you go about it if you want to tell the people who look at your pictures something about the feeling we get up here on the roof at dawn, with hardly a flier in sight, and the loneliness and this gloomy city below. We could be the last people on Uller—or the first. Oh, I wish—"

He glanced at her sharply. "What?"

"Nothing. Here comes the flier."

The plate in the roof slid back and the flier appeared on its elevator, looking rather like a pious insect with its vane-cases folded over its back. Lajos climbed in, took the food package and painting equipment and snapped them into a locker, then said, "Button in tight. I'm going to give her a rocket shot unless you think you want to look at the scenery below."

"No thank you. The scenery on this planet doesn't impress me. In fact, I could do without it for the rest of my life."

He fingered the controls and opened the key to the rocket fuel line. "Is that why you've decided not to go through with the marriage?"

"No, I— Oh, stop trying to fish around in my mind."

HIS only answer was to step on the power button, and Greta was jerked sharply into the buffers as the flier slanted upward with air screaming around it. The rocket cut out and the pressure eased as they began to tilt downward; Harkavy set the vane-openers to automatic and said, "You're right about the painting. It's up to the artist to convey every type of emotion—to find means to make absolutely anyone experience what he felt at the time. The only trouble is that I wouldn't know how to go about making a given member of the advanced group experience any emotion whatever."

"I'm a member of the advanced group."

"Only by heredity, and with a low temperament rating. One of the difficulties of our so-called civilization is that the capacity for emotion has been practically bred out of the upper scientific levels in the interest of obtaining eugenic qualities that will give greater intelligence. And if the advanced group succeeds in putting through the regulation making it impossible to refuse a marriage ordered by the Eugenic Committee, it will be worse than ever."

"I hadn't thought of it that way," said Greta. "But it did seem to me that the regulation would be—unjust."

There was a clicking as the helicopter vanes took over. Harkavy peered downward to get his bearings, took the wheel and said, "A desire for justice, in fact, even the concept of justice, is a purely emotional matter itself. Unscientific. Don't you remember studying about some of the archaic political states on Earth, where the elected non-scientific authorities could declare certain things were true or not, even prohibit scientific research along some lines?"

Greta said, "I should think that, feeling the way you do, you'd try to do something about it. The new marriage regulation, I mean. After all, your intelligence number is low enough to make you a policy-maker."

Harkavy shrugged. "Association politics doesn't interest me. Evolution will take care of the matter in time. Although if it's controlled as sharply as the advanced group wishes, man is certainly going to evolve into two subspecies, one species with all the intelligence and no emotion, and the other absolutely the reverse. In fact, I think we're some distance along that road now."

"You're a fatalist." She leaned over to look at the incredible sight of an Ullerian forest swimming up toward them, with its curious wilted-looking thin-trunked trees just breaking into the tenderest of green leaves at the tips of their branches, the sunlight touching the spicules of quartz in their trunks to a thousand changing colors, while here and there a dead tree stood like a single milky jewel.

The flier sank smoothly toward a cleared area in a valley between two hills, did a slight upward slant and came to rest on the slope. "Let's eat our breakfast inside," said Greta. "I don't mind glassine, but you'll need all the space in the hut for your painting things."

"All right. What's the menu?"

"I have no idea. The hostel put it up; I just told them I wanted two meals for two people, one of them a hungry man."

She produced the three cans marked for breakfast, turned the heating keys and began to lay disposable dishes on the table Harkavy detached from the wall.

"Continuing our former conversation," said Harkavy, "what both the pure and applied scientists have lost sight of is that the original purpose of science was to serve mankind as a whole. They look down on us psychs and barely allow us the name of scientists, but it's something we can't forget, because people are our raw material."

"Oh, I don't think the moderates have forgotten it," said Greta. "They just don't want all their researchers under the control of the advanced group, and for their interests. Here, try some of this. It smells delicious. Meat of some kind. By the way, there aren't any animals around here, are there?"

"Not likely to be," said Harkavy. "That is, not dangerous ones, although there might be a few little 'cone-cats around. The gonflar country is down toward the sea, and you don't usually find burex unless there are gonflars for them to prey on."

WHEN they finished the meal, Harkavy decided that the view from the opposite hill was better and got out his equipment to walk over. Greta accompanied him to the hilltop, but after he had set up his glassine hut and begun to work, he began answering her remarks with a series of grunts, so she went outside to wander among the trees and look at the mosses that crawled over the ground under them in patterns as intricate as snowflakes.

She could see quite a distance between the thin trunks so there wasn't any danger of getting lost, but she herself hardly realized how far she had gone until she heard a shout muted by distance and turned to see Harkavy waving her frantically toward him. As she ran toward him she became aware of a muffled roaring sound in the distance like the sea beating on a beach, and abruptly she was running into an increasing gusty rush of wind. A fallen opalescent log caught her foot, and down she went, with a sharp shard from one of the broken branches penetrating her cold-suit and cutting her knee, but she was up again in a minute and running. Out of the corner of her eye, she caught a flicker of something white, and then she was beside Harkavy.

"Too late," he said, pointing. The whole area between them and the hill where the flier stood was filled with tossing waves and beyond it toward the south a white crest was rushing, while the continually rising wind tore at them.

"What is it?" she asked.

"The spring bore. It's my fault; I forgot about it; I even forgot this was the right area for it."

"What's the spring bore?"

"You haven't been here long enough to learn about all the niceties of our climate. You know the poles freeze in winter; big ice-caps melt almost as large as those on earth. When they begin to melt in the spring, the rivers start running toward the central seas, but at first it's only a trickle here and there, because ice-jams form at their source-points. Then one day the water pressure behind gets to be too much for the ice-jam, and she goes out like that."

"Will it last long? Can we get back to the flier?"

"Can't tell how long. May have to stay here over night, maybe not. Let's get the hut braced, though. The winds that follow these bores are usually something."

He worked more rapidly than she would have imagined, picking up fragments of the quartz tree limbs and stacking them around the base of the invisible glassine hut. Greta limped after him until he stopped her with; "You'd better get inside and sit on my chair. Moving around isn't doing that cut on your knee any good, and the first aid kit's over in the flier. Here, wait—"

He ran rapidly down to the shore of the roaring torrent and returned with a piece of ice. "Here, put this on it. That will stop the bleeding."

"Isn't it silicious?" asked Greta.

"Not enough to worry about. Spring ice is pretty clear; you can even drink the water from it."

Greta said, "Ouch" at the touch of the ice, then, "Do you know, I was thinking about your luminescent colors and the effect of changing light. In math we have a series of equations known as the Weierstrass analytics, a development of Hamilton's work in optics. I think a formula could be worked out on that basis which would give you perfectly predictable results, even with luminescent colors."

Harkavy frowned. "I thought you pure mathematicians were disinterested in practical results," he said. Then, "It isn't just a matter of predictable results in a physical sense. We know pretty much what we're getting that way, even with luminescents. It's the resulting emotional reaction that concerns us as painters. That's where the whole quarrel with the advanced group lies. They aren't prepared to admit as a science anything that doesn't give a predictable result."

"Elementary school observation, Mr. Harkavy." "I know. I was clearing the ground. But I'm convinced that there is a real science of psychology, and the only way we can reach it is by way of the arts, by producing emotions through artistic means and then checking on how we got what we did."

She looked past him out through the glassine wall to where the arms of the rubbery trees were whipping in the wind. "I almost wish—Lajos, what's that?"

ALONG the direction of her pointing finger, among the trunks, a creature like a biologist's nightmare was shuffling toward them, its reptilian head low as it sniffed the ground, and its three pairs of squat legs moving in uneven undulations.

"Burax!" said Harkavy. "I said there wouldn't be any this far north. Well, I was wrong. He must have smelled the blood where you cut yourself. They've developed a taste for mammalian blood that makes them a little more dangerous than a flock of tigers."

He was working at the side of his painting-case, which dropped open to reveal a white object about a foot and a half long, surmounted by a tube which ended in a transparent conical noozle.

"What—" began Greta, as the burax, appearing to catch sight of them for the first time, lumbered forward in a clumsy charge. Harkavy snapped a gap in the glassine, and as the creature closed in, a jet of something white sprang from it, straight into the reptilian face and long jaws. The jet seemed to go right in; Greta saw that where it struck there was a bubbling that seemed to come from the very interior of the animal's head, its two middle legs clawed forward as the front legs doubled up, and it lay twisting and heaving outside the hut.

"What did you do to it?" asked Greta, contemplating that silent agony.

"Gave it a dose of pure hydrofluoric acid. They're just about indestructible to anything else. I'm afraid we're going to be chilly in here, though." He pointed to where the drip from the nozzle of the gun had cut a long series of slashes in the glassine wall, through which the chill was flowing into the hut.

VIII

LATER, talking to Frasser, Greta explained. "—And in the morning he waded over and brought back the flyer and here I am," she finished. "Chemistry isn't my branch, so I don't know quite how peculiar it is, but I do know it isn't usual."

"It's so damned unusual that I can't think of a good explanation offhand," said Frasser. "But it does hook up with a couple of other things."

"What sort of things?"

Frasser frowned, and his rather pop eyes opened a trifle wider. "Look here," he said, "how real is this painting of his?"

Greta sipped from her glass. "Very real. I've seen some of his pictures at the studio, and I saw him begin on one while we were on the trip. And they're good; not that I'm an art critic, but as he explained to me, he's working on the conveyance of emotion by means of pictures, and I think he's getting somewhere. I don't know any better way of telling it than saying that when the light shifts in one of them you seem to *feel*

something more than that—"

"You talk like a psych—or a low-level tech. However that's not the point. There isn't any chance, then, that the painting is a cover for some other form of activity?"

"It could be. After all—" she gave a little hard bark of a laugh"—I haven't been with him too many of his waking hours and comparatively few of his sleeping ones. He could be running half a dozen things on the side. Like that dancer. But why all the questions?"

"The night before you left Marius Rizzi went to Harkavy's studio and spent practically the entire night there. In connection with your story I think this makes it practically certain that they're up to some scientific activity together. And the only research projects Rizzi has registered with the Uller Council are in connection with carbon-nitrogen-silicone chain molecules, nothing at all about hydrofluoric acid."

"Then the project isn't authorized, whatever it is. Can't you bring charges before the Council?"

Paul Frasser made a mouth. "And take the chance that it's all strictly on the level and I'd run into a false accusation charge? No thanks; Marius Rizzi is a physical chemist and an 18. I'd have to know a lot more about what I was charging him with before I tackled a customer like that. But let's figure this out; you've been in Harkavy's quarters; what's the layout, and is there space enough to house a laboratory of any kind?"

Greta closed her eyes in an effort of memory. "It's down—one of the underground quarters. When you come off the elevator you're in a rather small square room that he uses for a reception room. On the left toward the back is the door of his studio, so." She traced an imaginary plan with her finger. "The studio runs all the way back; it's a big oblong room. Next to it, right behind the reception room, is the dining-room, and running the length of both of them, to the right of the reception room as you come in, is a long bedroom and living room, with shifting partitions and one of those antique fireplaces."

"No doors or sliding panels that might lead to more rooms?"

"Not off the reception room. It has doors in three walls and the elevator panel. Or the dining room either; that has three doors and the food delivery tube. And I don't think the studio. It would have to be pretty well concealed, and I can't imagine why he'd want to conceal it that carefully. There might be an entrance to another quarters through the bathroom or one of the closets off the bedroom; I never thought of looking."

Frasser said, "I think you better had. We want to be sure."

"But I've broken the acquaintance and given notice."

"I know. But this is so important we can't afford to overlook a thing. I'll tell you how it can be arranged. I'll have someone watch the place and notify you when he goes out, so you can slip in. There's every chance in the world that the door-lock is still tuned to your voice and even if it isn't and you have to get the building officer to let you in, there wouldn't be anything queer about your going to the quarters of an acquaintance. That's why you're the only one who can do it without arousing suspicion—his or anyone's."

GRETA shuddered a little. "I hate to think of how I'd explain myself if he came back and found me there. Why is it so important to find out whether he has a laboratory?"

"Merely because of what you've just been telling me. About some kind of gun that projects high-speed jets of hydrofluoric acid. Do you realize what that means?"

"No. What?"

"Taken in conjunction with the meeting with Rizzi it probably means that our young artist, our time-waster is going to have a try at Niflheim for beryllium, and that he's close to the solution

of the major problem. Do you see?"

"Work it out for me, Paul. I told you chemistry wasn't my branch."

"The trouble with Niflheim is staying alive. The atmosphere has a certain percentage of free fluorine, enough to kill you quick, mixed up with a weird collection of the gaseous fluorides of practically all the non-metals in existence. It's been sampled. That looks all right to start with because you can build a protective suit like a space suit out of metal and after the free fluorine has attacked the outer surface and formed a thin coating of fluoride, nothing more happens, just the way aluminum reacts with water-vapor in the air to a small extent. But there are rains on Niflheim and they consist mostly of hydrofluoric acid, which isn't very good for a protective suit, even when it's made of the Vang metal they use in rocket-tubes. The joints aren't very safe and one little crack could play hell with the man inside the suit.

"Besides, there's the little problem of seeing your way around. We just don't know of any glass or transparent plastic that would last more than a couple of hours in Niflheim's atmosphere. A man would be quite blind there, even if he were safe otherwise. The only way to be certain would be to build out of something that already has so much fluorine in it that it can't take on any more. Like Teflon."

"What's Teflon?"

For answer Frasser got up and went to the spool cabinet, extracted a spool and put it into the speaker. "Hubbard's list of elementary chemical compounds," it announced, and ejected the index strip, on which Frasser made his selection. The machine clicked and gurked. "Teflon," it said, "a plastic composed of very long chains of linked CF_2 units. Hardness 4.5. Tough. White to grayish in color, translucent in very thin sheets. Can be extruded and pressed into shapes at temperatures around 205 degrees. Easily machined, requiring no lubrication during the process. Subject to cold flow under continuous high pressure. As the carbon-fluorine bond is extremely strong, remains absolutely inert chemically at normal temperatures, and cannot be stuck to anything whatever. Known since the twentieth century."

FRASSER switched the machine off. "There you are," he said. "But notice that the man said translucent in very thin sheets, while you said the nozzle of Harkavy's gun was transparent. Sure about that?"

"I certainly am. It looked as though the liquid came from inside the thing and some kind of pressure were applied to it inside the nozzle and from another source."

"Could be. Good mechanical arrangement. They probably made it as a test piece, to see whether their material would stand up without leaking under service conditions. But I don't think there's much doubt that they've succeeded in producing a transparent form of teflon, and they probably have another, opaque form with greater hardness that working parts can be made of. That's Rizzi's doing, damn him."

Greta stirred in her seat. "There's something I don't understand," she said. "Why are he and Lajos keeping it so secret if they're really going to Niflheim and have the means? It would be of immense benefit to the whole of humanity if they could get at the beryllium. Any Council, even the central one, ought to be glad to authorize it."

Paul Frasser's smile was more like a snarl. "If you don't know the answer to that one, you're more emotionally romantic than I thought. For one thing, your father's little playmates aren't too anxious to have beryllium found. If interstellar travel stops, they'll stay right where they are on most worlds, sitting on top of the heap. For another thing, if Rizzi and Harkavy pull it off by themselves they'll gain so much credit and so many votes, right in the association, that they can practically write their own ticket. We won't even be able to

hold the moderates in line. And with a psych running things, we might as well go back to the old days when political officers controlled even scientists."

"I see."

"So the first thing is to find out where they're making the stuff, get the formula if possible, keep them from using it before we can take some action. It's too bad you broke the acquaintance now. You might have been able to make him talk."

Greta said, "We all make mistakes, don't we?" and stood up. "I'll stay in my quarters to hear from you about Lajos being out. Make it as soon as you can; I have my special travel permit, and want to be on my way back to earth."

"Oh, that reminds me," said Frasser. "Your adored parent seems to have become somewhat excited about your breaking off the acquaintance with Harkavy. While you were out on your little jaunt among the burax we got word that Roger Ingelhide is on his way here."

Greta stopped. "That's queer. He usually only does political errands for father. Like rounding up support for a new regulation or getting somebody disenrolled as a scientist."

IX

THE perpetual violent wind of Uller drove the rain in little hard level pellets that stung right through the transparent face-hood of Greta's raincoat as she climbed from the ground car, pressed the lever that would send it into the automatic garage and let herself into the weather-hall of the building where Lajos Harkavy had his quarters.

An old serv was guiding a cleaning machine down the hall. He smiled and lifted a hand in recognition, and Greta wished she hadn't been seen, but there was nothing she could do about it now. She felt her heart beating rapidly, and decided that this was what it must have felt like to be one of those persons who took other people's property—she couldn't remember the word for them—

back in the archaic ages before science took control and the Eugenics Committees bred anti-social behavior practically out of existence.

The elevator slid smoothly downward. Greta stepped across the narrow hall, approached the sonic plate and pronounced the phrases that would give it the combinations of sound that under the subtle analysis of the device would be as much her own as her finger-prints; "This is Greta Manning; one, two, three, five, six, why, piebald, gentian." Frasser had been right; the door slid back and the lights in Lajos' reception room came on.

He hadn't changed anything, but she had hardly expected him to. She turned into the bed and living room, touched the reception room lights to silence and stood for a moment, looking around in the dimmer radiance that flowed from walls and ceiling at her entrance. Right ahead Lajos had moved one of the partitions around the corner where the bed was, probably to use spray while he slept; there couldn't be any door in that corner. To her left another partition with an open swinging door in it permitted a glimpse of the fireplace. He had changed things there, too, making that part of the room into more of an intimate corner for reading, and when Greta went through the door, she saw that a projector was hung on the partition.

The fireplace itself might, just might conceal a panel leading to another apartment; if Lajos were clever enough to have covered up his scientific activity so well, he was clever enough to have thought of that. She stepped to it, touched the light to greater brilliance, and began examining the intricate carving of the mantelpiece for any detail that might indicate a door-button.

With the greatest clarity the speaker in the wall pronounced, "This is Lajos Harkavy; one, two, three, five, six, why, piebald, gentian."

Greta had just time to put the lights out with a panicky jab of her finger when the light in the reception room came up at the entry of someone and Lajos' voice said, "Come in. I think I can guarantee——" He stopped.

Another voice, somewhat heavier said, "Beg pardon?"

Lajos said, "Be comfortable and take off your cold-suit. I was saying that I had wired this place with detectors so that you need not worry about spy-rays. Privacy on Uller is expensive; we have so little outdoor life. Will you have a spray, or a drink or tobacco?"

Greta crouched and crept toward the back of the room, where at a pinch she might slip through into the dining room, blessing the softness of the silicoid floor.

The heavy voice said, "I do not myself indulge, but I would not find it disturbing if you wish to do so."

Lajos said, "You pure scientists seldom do. What can I do for you?"

In the dark Greta tripped on something and almost fell, but saved herself with the arm of a big chair.

SHE heard the heavy voice say, "Mr. Harkavy, I want you to judge the importance with which my mission is regarded by the fact that, even with the extremely restricted amount of interstellar travel available, I was alloted a reaction car for the sole purpose of coming out here to see you."

"I am honored, Mr. Ingelhide." (Greta could imagine the slightly malicious gleam in Lajos' eyes as he said this.) "You could always reach me on a closed beam circuit."

"This is not a matter that could be discussed in that way. Let us put it that it is a matter of negotiation."

There was a momentary silence in which each seemed to be waiting for the other to say something. Evidently Lajos won, for it was the heavy voice of Ingelhide that spoke first; "I am here as the personal representative of the President of the Association for the Advancement of Science."

"I am more than honored."

"His daughter has just given up her acquaintance with you."

"Yes. She decided we were not temperamentally suited for marriage with each other."

Ingelhide's voice was heavy with disapproval. "In our group I am afraid we cannot recognize the existence of temperamental difficulties as scientific. But I will not labor the point: The heart of the matter is that a certain situation has resulted."

"You mean the beryllium shortage?"

"You know a good deal, don't you, Mr. Harkavy? That is one aspect of it, yes. A certain group calling themselves the moderates, chiefly composed of applied scientists, are trying to make use of the difficulties caused by this shortage to make themselves dominant in the Association, that is, throughout civilization everywhere. We believe they intend to degrade both the pure scientists and the psychologists to the level of techs. I need not point out to you how dangerous this would be, for you personally, and for civilization as a whole."

"Go on."

"The test case will be the proposal for a new marriage regulation, making all marriages proposed by the Eugenics Committee compulsory. The moderates propose to defeat the regulation. As this will constitute a vote of no-confidence in the present Council, a new one would have to be elected, dominated by the moderates, and they would then proceed with the rest of their program."

Greta could hear Lajos give a little laugh. "Very ingenious, aren't they? But I don't see why you should come out here to tell me about this. I have no vote; I'm not even an adult, officially."

"That is what I came here for. The President of the Association authorizes me to say that it would be possible to pass a special regulation conferring adulthood on a man of your intelligence rating. The psychs would hardly oppose it, and with the help of the advanced group, there would only be a certain number of moderates in opposition."

"I see," said Lajos. "Provided I came out for the new marriage regulation afterward."

Ingelhide's voice was smooth. "Naturally, we would be cooperating. You would automatically have a seat on the Council. It might even be possible to have you given the rating of a pure scientist."

"I am more flattered than ever."

"As for the young lady in question, if it met with your approval, once the new marriage regulation was passed one of the first acts of the Eugenics Committee would be to pronounce a marriage between you and her eugenically desirable."

"You haven't overlooked a thing, have

THE ADVENTURES OF

IT SMELLS GRAND

AROMA SWEET AS ANY ROSE —

IT PACKS RIGHT

PACKS TO PLEASE YOU—
GOODNESS KNOWS!

you?" Greta held her breath until she almost strangled, waiting for what was coming next. It did not come at once; there was the click as the doorpanel to the studio slid back, the muffled sound of Lajos' footsteps and then his voice:

"Mr. Ingelhide, does this picture mean anything to you?"

"It appears to be a representation of two people standing on a cliff at twilight. Why, they're moving! And the twilight's getting darker!"

"That's the effect of luminescents. The painting hasn't anything else to say to you?"

Ingelhide's voice was slightly puzzled. "It is very skilfully rendered," he said tentatively.

GRETA heard Lajos sigh. "Thank you for the compliment. I came out here to Uller to paint it because this is the only world that would provide me with the necessary effects. And it is supposed to convey the terror of a failing and falling world, in which two people have no resource against the dark but each other. Either I have failed to make this clear, or you have not understood it. It doesn't matter. But surely you can see that you have as little understanding of the emotions that actuate me as I have of the calculations that actuate you. The answer to your proposal is no, and no again."

Ingelhide's voice took on a dangerous edge. "We may be forced to make other arrangements—"

"I have no doubt you will try. Now, listen to me. You think you are offering me the keys of the universe. Bah! I already have greater prospects than any you can dream of, and I shall not be indebted for their fulfillment to a group which intends to fasten a tyrannical stasis on mankind in the name of science. Good-bye, Mr. Ingelhide; I wish you a pleasant journey back to earth."

"If you feel that way about it—"

"I do. Good-bye."

There was the click of the elevator door-panel. Greta heard Lajos' feet go pad, pad, then she was suddenly bathed in light and his voice said, "You can come out now."

Her face flaming, but as boldly as possible, she walked through into the reception room. "I suppose you knew it was me, and not just anyone?"

"Of course. As I told that rather crude gentleman who brought your father's message, I have detectors on the place. The little box just over the door to the dining room, which you probably never noticed, reported that the lights had been on. Since you are the only other person for whom the door has been tuned—I must have that looked after, by the way—it was obvious that

[Turn page]

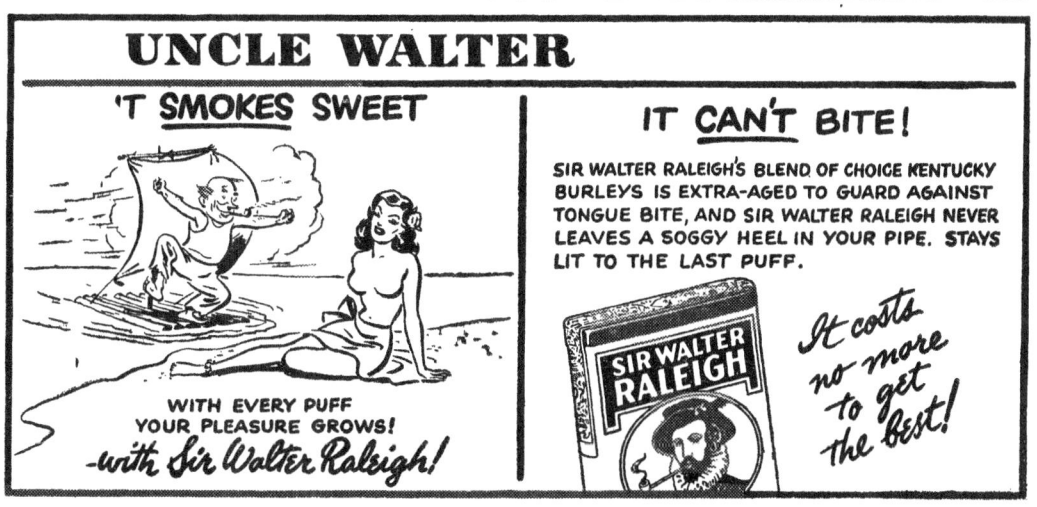

you had come to the place while I was out, and were still here. I thought something like that might happen when I found I was being followed on going out. That's why I hurried back."

Greta said coolly, "I'm surprised you didn't haul me out for Ingelhide's benefit."

"Oh, that would never do. You see, I know you're spying for the moderates, and I'd rather have you let them know exactly where I stand than turn you in to your father's group. He'd be likely to banish you to one of the less pleasant planets; has no emotion in his makeup, you know."

"Very chivalrous of you," said Greta, trying to make the remark sarcastic. "What makes you think I'm spying for the moderates?"

Lajos put his fingertips together. "First: you tried to plant a spy-ray on me. That's comprehensible in a girl who wants to know something about the man she is probably going to marry, but suspicious. Second: the same ship that brings you to Uller also brings Paul Frasser, an agent of the moderates, and although you have no contact with him on board, you visit his quarters after you arrive. Third: you break off the acquaintance for no assignable reason and at a most pecular time. Fourth: when we went on the trip to MacMurray Forest, you defended the moderates against the advanced group. Fifth: you slip into my quarters while I'm out to look for something. Did you find it, by the way?"

"Are you sure you're perfectly right on all those points, Mr. Harkavy? No, I didn't find it. May I go now?"

"As you wish." He touched the button for the doorpanel.

As she stepped through, she turned. "Good-bye, Lajos Harkavy. There's one thing about me, though. At least I don't cheat."

She saw his mouth gape in amazement behind the closing panel.

THE clerk at the hostel said Mr. Frasser was out and would be back late, but had left word that she was to wait if she came and gave her the key. Also an urgent closed-beam transcript had just come in for him; would she take it up?

Paul Frasser's suite had two rooms and a window, but the supply of reading spools seemed limited to technical material in fields that did not interest Greta, and the window offered no resources but the pitch-black clouded night of Uller, studded here and there with a trail of light as a flyer went past. There didn't seem to be much to do but sit down and think, so Greta did that for a while, wondering how much more Lajos knew and what he meant to do next. The latter seemed reasonably obvious; he was going to make a try for Niflheim and its beryllium. But he'd need a special permit to use a reaction car for interstellar travel in that case, and he'd have to get it either from the Uller Council or the main council of the Association, back on earth. And to get either one, he'd probably have to have moderate support in the councils.

Of course! thought Greta, when she got this far, that was the point. That was why Lajos hadn't done anything but let her go when he found her spying on him. He must be already in touch with some of the moderates, and his bold answer to Ingelhide had been deliberately given in her hearing, so she would take word of it back to Frasser. He was playing the same kind of game as the rest, and very cleverly, just as he had fooled her into thinking he was carrying on an honest acquaintance while he was really having an affair with that naked dancer.

Come, Greta, she told herself at this point, you mustn't get bitter, it's bad for your emotional stability. Where were we? Oh, yes, Lajos must have been in touch with the moderates. Then the closed-beam transcript she had brought up for Frasser would be an instruction from Shigemitsu and the other leaders back on earth about the new policy of cooperating with the psychs.

Without any sense of eavesdropping,

and because she had always been treated as one of the leaders of the group, Greta dropped the spool into the player. It gave the series of code clicks that indicated a closed-beam transmission which could be heard on just this one single player out of all those in the universe, and then Shigemitsu's voice came out, with that tiny suggestion of hissing accent that no one of Japanese ancestry ever quite lost:

"Your news is the best you could possibly send, and renders the success of our project practically certain if properly followed up. Of course, you will have perceived already that it is necessary to obtain the details of this new teflon process either from Rizzi or Harkavy before they can use it for a trip to Niflheim. The others are agreed with me that you are to stop at nothing, even primitive means, in obtaining it. Even if interstellar travel is restored on the fullest basis, our group cannot fail to be placed in charge of it, and this will permit us to have a majority in any council at any time. I do not think it will even be necessary to unseat the present council by a vote on the new marriage regulation; drop further efforts to persuade voting members along that line. I am glad you used your influence to obtain a special travel authorization for the girl. Her usefulness there is ended, and she is so emotional that she might cause trouble. We will have to dispose of her somehow when the program for the exclusion from the scientific rolls but that can be settled in due course. Remember that Rizzi is not dangerous in himself; it is Harkavy you must watch and work through."

A S THE message clicked off, Greta sat perfectly still, gripped by a kind of numb, cold horror. This was the result of her effort to make the world—the worlds—better places for people to live in. She was a puppet, a spy for a gang even more cynical than the advanced group headed by her father. At least the advanced group had ideals of a certain kind, even if she thought they were wrong, but Shigemitsu and his crew were after nothing but personal power, just as in the primitive period. There was no one, no one, she could trust. Of what use all the scientific advances man had made through centuries if they only led back, by another route, to the same cold struggle for power? Lajos had been right, and the result of careful breeding for intellectual attainment and emotional stability under the Eugenics Committees had turned most scientists into automata, whose only emotional satisfaction lay in making other people do as they wished.

The door opened and Paul Frasser came in, pulling open the fastenings of his cold-suit. "Hello," he said, without apologizing for keeping her waiting. "Did you find it?"

Greta said, "There's a closed-beam urgent for you on the player from Shigemitsu. He says you're to get Harkavy's teflon process at any cost, and to ship me home because I'm not useful here any more."

The tone she used made Frasser give her a sharp look. "Closed beam is supposed to insure the privacy of communications," he said.

"If you're going to have spies, you must expect them to spy on you, too. Especially when you cheat them," she replied, anger and despair mingling in her voice.

"Oh, come," he said, "this business of cheating is becoming what the psychs call a fixation with you. Look at matters rationally."

"I am. I have. And what I see is that you're no more interested in people as a whole than my father. You and your gang just wanted my help to get in control of interstellar communication—and then I'm not useful any more."

Frasser shrugged. "Somebody has to control it."

"Why not the councils of all the sciences, the way it's supposed to be done?"

"Somebody has to control them, too. To decide which line of scientific endeavor will yield the greatest benefit to humanity."

Greta said fiercely, "Yes, I've heard that before. Well, I'm through. When I get back to earth, I'll have nothing more to do with your 'movement.' No, wait, I will too. I'll denounce it in open Council or the convention of the Association."

"I think not."

"What will prevent me?"

"Your own rational view of the consequences. Stop and think about it logically and scientifically. You'll be accusing part of the Council and a good many members of the association of conduct inimical to the advancement of science. Do you think they'd rather listen to you or order you for examination as emotionally unstable? They wouldn't dare let the political power have such a chance to upset the system of scientific regulations."

HE WAS right, Greta realized as her first flush of anger began to cool, and she remembered the years of struggle it had taken to set science free from the control of the old political governments, in which not the most intelligent, but the most cunning came to the top—with their wars and jealousies and eugenically bad strains breeding unchecked. She said, "My father—"

Frasser cut her off with a laugh. "If he doesn't know all about it already, he's more of a fool than I think. The only trouble is that he can't identify the people mainly responsible. You know that. Try talking to him, and you'll find yourself on a transport for Freya as the first victim of his purge."

Greta dropped her head a little. "I just wish there was someone I could trust," she said slowly, and groped her way to the door.

Paul Frasser watched her go with something that was not quite a sneer on his face. He was about to put Shigemitsu's message through the player when something struck him, and he stepped rapidly across the room to the phone. "Hello," he told the hostel switchboard, "I want Derek Hyde, 316-422 on visual. Closed circuit."

There was a momentary wait before Hyde's head appeared on the plate, his hair tousled with sleep. "Hello, Hyde," said Frasser. "Nobody with you? Good. I know it's late and you love your rest, but this is an emergency. Remember that Manning girl, the good looking one we took to see Roselle La Blanche? She's been working with us, but I'm afraid we're going to have trouble, and it's got to be headed off. I sent her over to locate something at Harkavy's quarters. Don't know whether she found it or not, but she's just been here in a mood that makes me pretty certain she's going to turn sour."

Hyde had a finely chiseled face of the type that would have been called "aristocratic" in the old days. "What do you want me to do?" he asked. "Look her up and make love to her?"

"Stop being a fool and listen. There's just one danger, and that is that she'll go to Harkavy. I want you to get in touch with that building officer at his quarters, the one who gave you the tip-offs before, and have him notify you at once if she turns up there again. If she does, neither one of them must go out of the place alive and conscious."

Derek Hyde's aristocratic features appeared to be undergoing a revolution. The lines from nose to mouth pinched in and the eyebrows went up in the center. "But that's physical violence!" he squealed. "That's anti-social conduct! They'll psych me! They'll take away my mind!"

"Listen, you're playing in fast company now, up with the low intelligence number people. You do what I say, or something a lot worse than a psych will happen to you. I don't care how you arrange it, and I don't want to know, but that girl knows too much for the good of either of us, and she mustn't get it to Harkavy. Now move, before the roof falls in."

He snapped off the connection and

turned frowningly to listen to Shigemit-su's message.

XI

THE speaker said, "This is Greta Manning. May I come in?" Lajos Harkavy turned over in bed, snapped back the covers with one motion, dropped a night-suit around him with another, snapped the back-switch, said "Come," and stepped around the partition to meet her as the door of the reception-room slid back and its lights came on.

The hood of her cold-suit was back, but she had not taken it off; at the expression on her face, he checked any intention to make a light remark and motioned her to a seat. He said, "I'd like to spare you any embarrassment, but I'm afraid that as you came to see me, you'll have to speak first."

"All right," she said. Her voice was nearly toneless. "I had to come and tell you. I couldn't feel honest otherwise."

Lajos didn't sit down or say anything.

"You're not making it easy," she said.

"I beg your pardon." He stepped to the back of the room, turned a button and the place was filled with the faint scent of the pine mountains of earth. "It's not an emotional spray," he said, "merely a relaxer," and crossed to sit down opposite her. "Have you seen Malya."

"No. Yes. I came for something else." The spray was already taking effect, and she felt better. "I just wanted to let you know that when I took the job of —spying on you, I didn't have any idea of what was really going on."

"How do you mean?"

The girl made a gesture with one hand. "I wonder if you understand. I think you probably do, even if you won't say so. The reason I wanted to help the —the moderates was because my father's group wanted to make the pure scientists—oh, you know, a privileged caste, and I didn't like it, even if I do rate as a pure scientist."

"I know. We talked about that back on earth. In the park beside the Hudson."

"And you told me that interstellar travel was going to end very soon."

"Yes," said Harkavy, "I told you that. I told it to you deliberately, and it wasn't quite true, because I thought you were in the clear and I didn't want to see you get mixed up in the fight. There isn't much mercy for anyone in it. Actually, there will be enough beryllium for a small amount of space travel for them foreseeable future. But the people who control it are going to control all the worlds. They can always send enough of their own group in to win a vote in the Council."

Greta said; "That's what I wanted to tell you. The moderates are as bad as the advanced group. All they want is to control. They want to put the rest of us down to tech status. And Paul Frasser's one of them."

"I know it."

"And send anyone who stands against them to some place like Freya."

"I know that, too."

"All right, did you know Toijiru Shigemitsu was one of them, too?"

Lajos changed his position. "No, I didn't. He has always behaved publicly like a real moderate, not a member of the group. Thank you."

"All right," said Greta, "now let me ask you a question. Are you and Rizzi planning a trip to Niflheim for beryllium? Because that's what Shigemitsu thinks, and he's going to do anything he possibly can to prevent it."

Lajos stood up and walked across the floor, his forehead set in a frown. "If I could be sure. . . ."

"Of me? If I could be sure of you. How do I know that what you told Ingelhide was just to impress me? Just as when you told me that interstellar travel was going to stop completely, only it isn't."

"We don't seem to be getting any-where—"

The red light beside the door flashed.

Lajos stepped over to it and switched the button to the "In" position, and the voice said; "Urgent. Package delivery."

AT THE sound of the click Lajos opened the delivery box in the wall to reveal a small container in dark plastic. "I wonder what that could be," he said, and pressed the opening slit. The box split; out on the table leaped a bright-colored something like a many-hearted jewel which turned and twisted urgently. In a flash Greta leaped from her seat, dashed it to the floor and stamped on it, while Lajos stood looking at where it had been with slack face and a foolish smile. Greta slapped him, hard. "Come out of it!" she said.

Lajos put one hand slowly up to his cheek, then turned to her, blinking. "What happened?" he said. "What was it?"

"A topological knot. They're hypnotic unless you know enough about pure mathematics to keep from being caught by them." She lifted her foot. "I think it's safe for you to look at it now, though. It wasn't made of very good material, and I've bent it out of shape. They use them as tests in higher mathematical training."

Lajos gazed at the object curiously, but did not attempt to pick it up. "It occurs to me," he said, "that you could just as easily have let me be hypnotized by that thing. I'd have done almost anything you told me, wouldn't I?"

"Yes."

HE GRINNED wryly. "In any case, I'll have to trust you to a certain extent. Sending that thing here means that someone is disturbed enough about what I'm doing to be willing to take a chance on having his mind wiped out for anti-social behavior. It also means there'll be a follow-up, and whoever it is will be plenty dangerous."

"I think I know who it is," said Greta. Frasser. Shigemitsu told him to stop at nothing to get your transparent teflon. I told him about it."

"I—"

The voice plate, in firm tones, said; "This is a Regulator Tech. Lajos Harkavy, you are to open the door at once."

"He thinks he's got you under," whispered the girl.

There was a silence from outside which seemed to prolong itself unbearably. Harkavy suddenly bounced through the side door into the studio, and was as rapidly back with the painting case and began unsnapping it just as the voice plate ejaculated; "Lajos Harkavy, I shall be forced to violate your privacy unless you admit me at once."

"Here," he said, thrusting the queer-looking weapon he had used in the Mac-Murray Forest into the girl's hands. "You work it with this lever. Hold him off if he gets in. I'm going to call for help—if they haven't cut the circuit."

The crack of an impulse-whip sounded against the door panel and a six-inch bulge appeared in it, as Harkavy bounded into the studio again. *Wham!* The budge widened and a crack ran across it. *Slam!* The crack became a gap through which a red glow showed as the next charge crashed into the door, splitting it right across. Greta crowded back toward the studio door to avoid the shock of the next one. Wham- bango! It sent the fragments of the door flying, and part of the charge tore into a chair across the reception room.

Into the gap stepped Derek Hyde, the impulse-whip under his arm.

"Where's Harkavy?" he demanded.

"Right here." Greta felt him beside her. "But you needn't worry about me. That weapon the young lady has is loaded with enough hydrofluoric acid to burn a hole right through you."

"I'll take my chance on that," said Hyde and raised the whip.

"Let him have it!" cried Harkavy.

"It's violence! I can't!" moaned the girl, and collapsed as Harkavy threw her to the floor, tumbling across her to avoid the charge that spurted into the studio and tore something from the wall with a crash.

Harkavy caught just a glimpse as the impulse-whip was lowered to finish them . . . and something hit Hyde from behind. The machine dropped from under his arm and an expression of the most intense surprise came across his face as he stood stock-still, utterly frozen, weapon under arm, finger on trigger. The next moment the place was swarming with half a dozen Regulator Techs, paralyzers in hand, and with Marius Rizzi frowning through the group.

ONE of the Regulators said; "Get that impulse-whip, Laurie. This is about the worst case of violence I've ever seen, and I think we better take him along without releasing anything but the legs."

Rizzi helped Greta up as one of the Regulators ran the release mechanism over Hyde's legs and shepherded him clumsily toward the elevator. Harkavy said; "Marius, you were certainly the god from the machine. I was trying to phone you when that maniac started breaking in, but I couldn't reach you. What in the nine worlds persuaded you to show up just at this time, and with a bodyguard."

Rizzi said; "Our little friend—" and then stopped and looked at Greta.

"It's all right," said Harkavy. "She's on our side."

Rizzi flashed a frown, but went on; "Our little friend Roselle—"

"Roselle!" cried Greta.

"Roselle la Blanche is one of our very best agents," said Harkavy, calmly.

"Lajos! Did you know it was because of her that I broke the acquaintance? They told me you had a connection with her."

"I do, but not the kind they meant. Go on, Marius, this sounds important."

"Our friend Roselle called and said Hyde had called her in a state of considerable excitement. He said he was being forced into an act of violence, and if he didn't come through, he wanted her to have his belongings. Well, the act of violence had to be against one of us, and as you had been watched and I hadn't, I got busy with a friend of mine in the Regulator office and came over here."

Harkavy said; "Let's go into the living room away from that wreck of a door and work this out. I don't like the implications."

He led the way through to the seats in front of the fireplace, seated himself and said; "This is Frasser's crowd; the moderates. Greta was working for them until she found out what they were really up to, and she tells me they know about your transparent teflon. That must be what they're after." -

"I told them about it," said Greta. "And then a closed beam came through from Shigemitsu on earth, telling Frasser not to stop at anything."

"I don't think he needed the encouragement," said Harkavy. "However, the question is what happens next. I don't think we can really pin anything on Frasser over this irruption of Hyde's. He'll have the guy pre-conditioned not to break under questioning, and even if he does, Frasser can always claim he exceeded instructions. And Frasser isn't the only man the moderates have on Uller. I'd rather let him alone and watch him than have them transfer the executive to someone we don't know about yet."

"May I speak?" said Greta. "There's a point that occurs to me. When they sent me here, that night, it was to find your laboratory and either have you up for unauthorized research or get the teflon process for themselves. Now Hyde comes in here and tries to blow you apart. It seems to me that this represents a change in emphasis from wishing to use the stuff themselves to preventing you from using it, and that's something you'll have to take into account."

"I believe you're right," said Rizzi. "And that means we'll have to work fast, before they or the advanced group can put a crimp in us from the Central Council. We only have two of the suits ready, but I think that gives us enough to just make it, if—"

"If what?" asked Greta.

"If we can get the travel authorization and the reaction car."

"You don't have to have it if you'll take me with you," said Greta. "I have a special authorization that was given to me when I broke the acquintance."

"I don't know that I care for that idea," began Harkavy, but Rizzi put out a hand. "I'm in favor of it. The fact that the moderates are onto our plan means that we wouldn't have much chance of getting away with a big ship and a heavy load in any case. A reaction car will just hold three, one to handle the machine and two to work outside, and all we need is a sample of the stuff, not a cargo. Also, I have my pilot's license. But there are problems."

"Such as?" said Greta.

"We'll have to line the air-lock of the car with teflon and arrange a pressure-gear to clear it of fluorine after use. That isn't difficult in a technical sense with the new process, and it won't take long, but the minute we start work, we're advertising where we're going, and I'm afraid Frasser will use the opportunity to pull something on us."

XII

MASCARIADES was the name of the captain of the port, and by ancestry he was a Greek. At the present moment he looked acutely unhappy, although his control tower had been run up to afford an exceptionally fine view of the port and the weather was, for Uller, uncommonly pleasant.

"I am very sorry," he said, "but in view of the complaint that you are about to make a journey to a point other than that covered by your papers, I cannot give you a clearance or furnish you with fuel."

"Who made the complaint?" asked Greta.

"Don't waste time," said Rizzi. "We know who made it. I'm the pilot of record, Mr. Mascariades, and therefore the ship's captain. What evidence is there to support the complaint?"

"The fact that you have altered the air-lock of the car to resist a non-terrestrial type atmosphere."

"You know an awful lot, don't you?" said Rizzi. "I think—"

"Wait a minute," said Harkavy. "That's not the way to handle this, Marius. Mr. Mascariades, will you get us a phone connection with the Council executive office? On visual."

"Certainly," said the captain, his relief showing in his voice, and turned to the instrument. In a moment a squarish face appeared on the screen, and a voice said; "Council Executive; Toller speaking."

"Mr. Toller," said Harkavy. "I am one of the passengers on reaction car VAK-321, authorized journey for Miss Greta Manning. We have just been refused clearance on the ground that our papers do not show the correct destination. I beg to submit that the destination is Earth, as stated, but we intend to make a stop-over at Niflheim."

The square face showed no sign of relaxing. "The Uller Council has already been apprised of that fact. It cannot authorize a clearance for Niflheim."

"Why not?"

"Because valuable equipment belonging to the Association will not be allowed to enter so corrosive an atmosphere."

"We have protected the airlock of the car. Exterior protection is unnecessary."

"Your unsupported statement is insufficient. The council has considered this question in view of information reaching it, and has decided that an analysis of the protective coating will be required."

Harkavy said; "That should be simple —" but Rizzi put a hand on his arm. "Just a moment," he said. "May we call back?"

"Certainly," said Toller, and the connection was abruptly broken.

Rizzi plucked at Harkavy's arm, pulling him a little aside. "It won't do," he said. "Frasser is a perfectly competent physical chemist. With an analysis of our transparent teflon he could duplicate it just about as fast as he could set up the apparatus."

"I see. And then he'd keep us here on some other pretext while he made the Niflheim exploration a general Association project with himself at the head of it. Very neat." Harkavy turned; "Mr. Mascariades, will you excuse us for a moment? We need to confer in view of the situation."

"Gladly," said the port captain. "You can use my inner office there. It is sound-proofed and has no spy ray—unless someone has installed one recently." He took on an anxious look. "Believe me, Mr. Harkavy, we techs will do anything permitted by the regulations to help you out."

WHEN they were in the office with Rizzi perched on a desk and the other two in the seats, Harkavy said; "Maybe you can suggest something, Greta. The way this thing is rigged, Frasser can get the transparent teflon process by an analysis. We should have lined that air-lock with opaque, but it's a little late to think of that now, and besides it would make the controls hard to get at."

The girl said; "Wouldn't the logical thing be to appeal from the Council to the general body of the Uller Association? There ought to be enough psychs and fair-minded applied scientists in it to give you a majority."

"There are two reasons why that won't work out," said Harkavy. "One is that we aren't exactly coming to court with clean hands after trying to slip away, so we couldn't be sure of holding the majority in line for a special, un-authorized project. The other is even more so; Frasser and his merry companions would appeal to Central Council back on earth, and either the advanced group would demand the new marriage regulation as the price of letting it go through, or they'd make it a Central

Council project. What we have to do is get there first and make the demonstration ourselves. It's the only way Marius and I can get enough promotion and backing. He'll have to take over if I can't be declared adult and take my place in the rankings."

Greta had been frowning. Now she said; "Would it help if it could be proved that the lining would stand Niflheim's atmosphere *without* making a chemical analysis?"

"It would help an awful lot," said Rizzi. "Even the moderates would find it hard to think up another objection in time. As I understand the captain out there, all we have to furnish is proof, it doesn't matter what kind. If it can be done."

"I think it can," she said, and stood up. "I want a spectroscopic light projector and a recorder for it. Also an electron microscope scalded in angstroms. And samples of fluorine and hydrofluoric acid."

"Those you can have," said Rizzi, "and the executive will have to send inspectors if you're going to make a test. But you'll probably get Frasser along with them."

They did; accompanied by techs bearing the equipment and a pair of representatives from the Council executive, one of them the square-faced Toller, the other a melancholy looking man bearing the name of Senef. Frasser greeted the others with the calm courtesy demanded of scientists in the presence of the lower ratings, and it was not until they stood before the opened door of the air-lock with Greta adjusting the projector to play on it that he said; "What do you propose to do?"

"I don't know that I care to tell you," said Greta. "Do you have official status to ask?" She turned to one of the techs. "I want the microscope set in phase to catch the reflection from the metal surface under the coating, and the recorder to pick up the result. Can you do that?"

"Miss Manning." It was Toller. "I have the official status to ask, and I do ask what you propose to do." Behind him Harkavy and Rizzi exchanged glances.

"Very well. I propose to demonstrate mathematically that this coating is impervious to the conditions on Niflheim."

Frasser said; "Gentlemen, I submit that this is absurd. A simple chemical analysis—"

"Would prove that the coating is impervious to fluorine under the conditions on Uller, not on Niflheim. Chemistry isn't my branch, but I do know you can't reproduce the Niflheim conditions in a laboratory. They're too complex."

"I don't think mathematical proof would be acceptable."

The melancholy Senef spoke for the first time. "The Council's regulation asked for proof but did not specify the nature of it. You have given us a good deal of trouble already, Mr. Frasser, and I am afraid you will have to be bound by our decision." Once more Harkavy and Rizzi exchanged glances.

"All right," said Greta to one of the techs. "Cut in the power. No, that's not quite right. There's a fadeout toward the UV. Can you get that set? There; it looks as though it's coming through correctly now. Record, and then move the projector slowly along."

GRETA tripped the holder and the record came out, a long band bearing a series of waving intricate curves. "Now will you run light tests on those samples of fluorine and hydrofluoric, and bring the records to me in the control tower, while I analyze this one?"

She led the way across the field past the firing pits to the control. When the group had gathered around the table in Mascariades' office, she spread the record of the light test out.

"Now, gentlemen," she said, "these curves represent the passage of light of different wave-lengths through the lining material. It went through twice, but that needn't concern us. Notice that it isn't a straight line, as you might expect, but a wavy curve; the different

wave-lengths of light encountered varying resistances from the molecules of the material."

"The phenomenon is a familiar one," observed Toller.

"I know," said Greta. "Now as far as a mathematician is concerned a wave is not a picture of something; it's a graphic method of expressing a periodic function. I'm going to reverse the process here and derive the function from the graph. The grid in the record will give us our coordinates. Have you got a hand calculator and a sheet of paper?"

She wrote rapidly as the figures ticked in the calculator, then turned to the two Council executives. "Observe that this function has a variable in it, due to the molecules of the lining being affected differently by light of different wave-lengths; and that as it progresses evenly where the record runs out into the infra-red and UV at the two ends, it is probably an infinite series. Since that is the case, the values of the variable, z, can only be described by a Weierstrass analytic power series."

Toller turned to Senef; "Is that correct? In astronomy we don't deal in this sort of thing."

Senef said; "It's correct enough; almost elementary. But I don't see what you expect to prove by it, Miss Manning. The series is convergent."

"You will in a minute," said the girl. "Ah, here's the record on those other two tests now. Let's take the fluorine one first. The one for the acid is just a check." Again she wrote and the calculator clicked. She handed the result to Senef. "Will you glance that over and see if it isn't correct? I want you to notice that it's another convergent series. That is, it approaches a finite number."

Senef's melancholy features took on a touch of glee. "I think I see what you're driving at. Yes."

"But if we combine the two," said Greta, and wrote again, "the result is a new series, and as you will see, it's divergent. It reaches to infinity; that is, the only point at which a combination of fluorine and the lining material could take place would be infinity."

Senef patted his hands together softly. "Admirable!" he said. "Thoroughly convincing. Toller, this is the proof we asked for. We probably should have known better than to doubt people of this order of intelligence."

"If you're satisfied—" began Toller.

"I'm not," said Paul Frasser.

Senef faced him. "I do not know that your opinions are a factor. Captain Mascariades, you may give this car an immediate clearance and a supply of fuel adequate for reaching Earth with a stop-over at Niflheim."

XIII

T HE meeting is open," announced President Manning, and the twenty-two members of the Central Council of the Association for the Advancement of Science stopped their low buzz of conversation and settled back.

"We still have pending the matter of the new marriage regulation," Manning said. "In the interests of—"

Old Henrik Kool raised his hand and said; "Floor."

"Pending business should be disposed of first."

Kool said; "I appeal from the decision of the chair. I have new business of such urgency that until it is disposed of we cannot deal properly with the pending business, and indeed the attitude of this body toward it may be altered by a change in the Council's composition."

"Please record ballots on the appeal," said Manning, and turned to face the voting board where the balloting done by keys in the arms of the seats was automatically recorded. "Two first rate scientists in favor of the appeal, six votes; two second rate, four votes; nine third rate, nine votes; total nineteen out of thirty-five. The appeal is supported. Mr. Kool, state your new business."

"I wish to present Lajos Harkavy,

BC-11-71, who has succeeded in reaching Niflheim and returning with proof that it contains ample supplies of beryllium to last the whole system for many hundreds of years of unrestricted interstellar travel, and that it can be handled safely."

"Is there any confirmation of the facts?" asked Manning, as calmly as though he did not know what was coming.

A man near the middle of the room raised his hand. "The chemical section confirms," he said. "Not only was a quantity of high-grade beryllium ore brought back, but also optical crystals of calcium fluoride of high indicated value."

"You may present," said Manning.

Kool stepped to the door and admitted Harkavy, Greta and Rizzi, leading them to seats at the front of the council room. When they were seated he faced the group. "In view of the achievement of Lajos Harkavy, I ask a seat on this Council for him, with the rank of first rate scientist; and I ask a seat for Marius Rizzi, his assistant, with the rank of third rate scientist."

A woman with dark hair, one of Manning's advanced group, claimed the floor and said; "Objection. If Rizzi made the discoveries, he should be promoted, but not Harkavy."

Kool said; "Mr. Rizzi, will you tell us about it."

Rizzi stood up. "The process by which protective plating for use in a fluorine atmosphere was developed was entirely due to Harkavy. I furnished only the laboratory and technical assistance."

The objector remained on her feet. "Unauthorized research!"

Harkavy spoke for the first time. "The research was done on Uller. That's why I went there. It's an outer, class C planet, and no authorization is required, provided only local materials are used."

The woman sat down, but another man raised his hand. "I have an objection as a member of the Eugenics Committee. According to our records, Mr. Harkavy is not an adult, and therefore cannot have either the rating you ask or a seat on this Council."

"I will move a regulation by this body to declare him adult," said Kool. "In view of attainments beyond those of anyone here, it is deserved."

The objector looked at a note and clung to his point. "According to the records, Mr. Harkavy lacks two years of the required age. If we are to make special regulations in individual cases, we might as well not have any regulations at all. It is hopelessly unscientific. Science admits of no exceptions."

Harkavy stood up. "May I speak? I could name a few exceptions science admits, and I can name one in the regulations. When a person of my age has made a marriage authorized by the Eugenics Committee, he is assumed to be stable enough to be declared adult."

"But you're not married. You'e not even on acquaintance."

"Oh, yes I am. Ask Marius Rizzi if you wish."

Rizzi said; "As captain of a ship in deep space, I was authorized to perform marriages, even when not authorized. Of course, there were only three of us aboard, and it wasn't much of a ceremony, but when they asked me, I could not very well refuse—could I?"

In the applause and murmurs that ran through the group it was a couple of minutes before Henrik Kool could get enough attention to say; "In the light of the evidence before us, I do not think there can be any objection to voting the regulations I have asked."

There was not.

WILDSIDE PULP CLASSICS: PULP FACSIMILE SERIES

Series editor: John Gregory Betancourt

#1: *Spicy Mystery Stories* (August 1935)
Includes Robert Leslie Bellem, Atwater Culpepper, Ellery Watson Calder, Carl Moore, E. Hoffman Price, Arthur Wallace, and more.

#2: *Ghost Stories* (June 1931)
Stories by Conrad Richter (author of The Light in the Forest*) and E. & H. Heron featuring psychic detective, Flaxman Low.*

#3: *Spicy Mystery Stories* (February 1937)
Features Robert Leslie Bellem, Lew Merrill (Victor Rousseau) Hugh Speer, Justin Case (Hugh B. Cave), & many others!

#4: *Strange Tales #7* (January 1933)
Features Hugh B. Cave's classic "Murgunstrumm," as well as stories by Robert E. Howard, Henry S. Whitehead, and many more.

#5: *The Black Mask #2* (May 1920)
2nd issue of classic mystery mag, where hardboiled fiction was born!

#6: *Tales of Magic and Mystery* (February 1928)
Legendary rare early fantasy magazine!

#7: *The Phantom Detective #1* (February 1933)
The premiere issue of the detective-hero pulp!

#8: *Submarine Stories* (March 1930)
Rare pulp magazine, stories and articles about (what else?) subs!

#9: *Sinister Stories #1* (Feb 1940)
The first issue of this "weird menace" pulp!

#10: *The Thrill Book* (Sept. 1, 1919)
The facsimile reprint from this legendary rare pulp magazine!

#11: *The Spider* (March 1940)
Includes the "Spider" novel Slaves of the Laughing Death!

#12: *Spicy Adventure Stories* (Dec. 1939)

- -

Please send me the following books, for which I enclose payment. (Or order online with a credit card at www.wildsidepress.com, or through your favorite online bookseller or pulp deather.)

- Spicy Mystery Stories (Aug.1935) - $19.95
- Ghost Stories (June 1931) - $19.95
- Spicy Mystery Stories (Feb. 1937) - $19.95
- Black Mask #2 (Jan. 1920) - $19.95
- Tales of Magic & Mystery (Feb. 1928) - $19.95
- Phantom Detective #1 (Feb. 1933) - $19.95
- Submarine Stories (Mar. 1930) - $19.95
- Sinister Stories (Feb 1940) - $19.95
- The Thrill Book (Sept 1. 1919) - $19.95
- The Spider (March. 1940) - $19.95
- Strange Tales #4 (Mar. 1932) - $15.00
- Strange Tales #7 (Jan. 1933) - $15.00
- Spicy Adventure (Dec. 1939) - $19.95

Mail to: Wildside Press
9710 Traville Gateway Dr. #234
Rockville, MD 20850
Online: www.wildsidepress.com

Name: _____

Address:_____

Address:_____

U.S. shipping: $3.95 for 1-2 books, $1 per additional book.
Other countries: please see www.wildsidepress.com

www.ingramcontent.com/pod-product-compliance
Lightning Source LLC
Chambersburg PA
CBHW081148170626
46809CB00010B/3143